GRADE **5**

The Adventures of Sherlock Holmes

福爾摩斯

Original Author　Sir Arthur Conan Doyle
Adaptors　　　Louise Benette, David Hwang
Illustrator　　　Kalchova Irina

1000

MP3

Let's Enjoy Masterpieces!

All the beautiful fairy tales and masterpieces that you have encountered during your childhood remain as warm memories in your adulthood. This time, let's indulge in the world of masterpieces through English. You can enjoy the depth and beauty of original works, which you can't enjoy through Chinese translations.

The stories are easy for you to understand because of your familiarity with them. When you enjoy reading, your ability to understand English will also rapidly improve.

This series of *Let's Enjoy Masterpieces* is a special reading comprehension booster program, devised to improve reading comprehension for beginners whose command of English is not satisfactory, or who are elementary, middle, and high school students. With this program, you can enjoy reading masterpieces in English with fun and efficiency.

This carefully planned program is composed of 5 levels, from the beginner level of 350 words to the intermediate and advanced levels of 1,000 words. With this program's level-by-level system, you are able to read famous texts in English and to savor the true pleasure of the world's language.

The program is well conceived, composed of reader-friendly explanations of English expressions and grammar, quizzes to help the student learn vocabulary and understand the meaning of the texts, and fabulous illustrations that adorn every page. In addition, with our "Guide to Listening," not only is reading comprehension enhanced but also listening comprehension skills are highlighted.

In the audio recording of the book, texts are vividly read by professional American actors. The texts are rewritten, according to the levels of the readers by an expert editorial staff of native speakers, on the basis of standard American English with the ministry of education recommended vocabulary. Therefore, it will be of great help even for all the students that want to learn English.

Please indulge yourself in the fun of reading and listening to English through *Let's Enjoy Masterpieces*.

亞瑟・柯南・道爾爵士

Sir Arthur
Conan Doyle
(1859–1930)

Sir Arthur Conan Doyle was born on May 22, 1859, in Edinburgh, Scotland. From an early age, he received a strict Spartan education. Influenced by his mother Mary Doyle, who had a passion for books and was a master storyteller, Arthur loved to read and compose.

He studied at the School of Medicine at Edinburgh University and met a number of future authors who were also attending the university, such as James Barrie and Robert Louis Stevenson. However, the man who most impressed and influenced Arthur was one of his teachers, Dr. Joseph Bell. The good doctor was a master at observation, logic, deduction, and diagnosis. All these qualities were later to be found in the persona of the famous detective Sherlock Holmes.

A couple of years into his studies, Arthur decided to try his pen at writing short stories. Since he especially respected Edgar Allen Poe and Emlie Gabriao, he wrote mystery stories and was completely immersed in creating his own vibrant characters. He finally created the most famous detective of all, Sherlock Holmes.

In 1887, starting with *A Study in Scarlet*, Arthur began publishing mysteries, wherein Holmes and Dr. Watson take active roles. Afterwards, he presented short stories in monthly magazines where he was well received by readers, which led to his popularity as a writer.

In 1892, he compiled those stories into *The Adventures of Sherlock Holmes*. He wanted to conclude the Holmes Series in 1894 with one last story, "*The Memories of Sherlock Holmes.*" However, acting on a request from readers, he again published *The Hound of the Baskervilles* in 1902. Afterwards, he wrote *The Return of Sherlock Holmes* and other stories to continue the series.

In 1902, he participated in the Boer War as an army surgeon and was knighted for distinguished service in war. Arthur Conan Doyle died on July 7, 1930, surrounded by his family. His last words before departing for "the greatest and most glorious adventure of all," were addressed to his wife.

The Adventure of the Speckled Band

One day, twin sisters living with their father encounter a mysterious case, and the older sister was killed. The younger sister, Helen, fears her life is in jeopardy and visits Holmes to ask for help. Intuitively aware of who the criminal is, Holmes sneaks into Helen's house. The thing that appears in the room was . . .

The Adventure of the Blue Carbuncle

The case begins as the doorman of Holmes's apartment accidentally picks up a goose and a hat on his way home from a Christmas party. A brilliant blue gem is in the stomach of the goose. Many people wonder how a gem could be placed in the goose's stomach.

A Scandal in Bohemia

The king of Bohemia personally visits Holmes and asks him to get back a picture that he took with his love in his youth. To solve the case, Holmes visits the king's old flame, and in a moment of bewilderment, he finds himself serving as a groomsman in her wedding. Will Holmes be able to get the picture back?

HOW TO USE THIS BOOK
本書使用說明

1 Original English texts

It is easy to understand the meaning of the text, because the text is rewritten according to the levels of the readers.

2 Explanation of the vocabulary

The words and expressions that include vocabulary above the elementary level are clearly defined.

3 Response notes

Spaces are included in the book so you can take notes about what you don't understand or what you want to remember.

4 One point lesson

In-depth analyses of major grammar points and expressions help you to understand sentences with difficult grammar.

🎧 *Audio Recording*

In the audio recording, native speakers narrate the texts in standard American English. By combining the written words and the audio recording, you can listen to English with great ease.

Audio books have been popular in Britain and America for many decades. They allow the listener to experience the proper word pronunciation and sentence intonation that add important meaning and drama to spoken English. Students will benefit from listening to the recording twenty or more times.

After you are familiar with the text and recording, listen once more with your eyes closed to check your listening comprehension. Finally, after you can listen with your eyes closed and understand every word and every sentence, you are then ready to mimic the native speaker.

Then you should make a recording by reading the text yourself. Then play both recordings to compare your oral skills with those of a native speaker.

HOW TO IMPROVE
READING ABILITY
如何增進英文閱讀能力

① *Catch key words*

Read the key words in the sentences and practice catching the gist of the meaning of the sentence. You might question how working with a few important words could enhance your reading ability. However, it's quite effective. If you continue to use this method, you will find out that the key words and your knowledge of people and situations enables you to understand the sentence.

② *Divide long sentences*

Read in chunks of meaning, dividing sentences into meaningful chunks of information. In the book, chunks are arranged in sentences according to meaning. If you consider the sentences backwards or grammatically, your reading speed will be slow and you will find it difficult to listen to English.

You are ready to move to a more sophisticated level of comprehension when you find that narrowly focusing on chunks is irritating. Instead of considering the chunks, you will make it a habit to read the sentence from the beginning to the end to figure out the meaning of the whole.

③ Make inferences and assumptions

Making inferences and assumptions is part of your ability. If you don't know, try to guess the meaning of the words. Although you don't know all the words in context, don't go straight to the dictionary. Developing an ability to make inferences in the context is important.

The first way to figure out the meaning of a word is from its context. If you cannot make head or tail out of the meaning of a word, look at what comes before or after it. Ask yourself what can happen in such a situation. Make your best guess as to the word's meaning. Then check the explanations of the word in the book or look up the word in a dictionary.

④ Read a lot and reread the same book many times

There is no shortcut to mastering English. Only if you do a lot of reading will you make your way to the summit. Read fun and easy books with an average of less than one new word per page. Try to immerse yourself in English as often as you can.

Spend time "swimming" in English. Language learning research has shown that immersing yourself in English will help you improve your English, even though you may not be aware of what you're learning.

CONTENTS

Before You Read

Sherlock Holmes

Sherlock Holmes is one of the greatest and most famous detectives[1] in the world. He can figure out[2] many things about people just by looking at a piece of their clothing. His powers of observation[3] and deduction[4] are incredible[5] and he uses them well to solve mysteries[6] that seem unsolvable[7]. He offers his skills for good people in trouble[8]. This has made him famous.

Dr. Watson

Dr. Watson is Holmes' oldest friend. He is not as smart as Holmes, and usually cannot figure out what Holmes is up to[9]. However, Holmes likes to have Dr. Watson around, perhaps as a "sounding board[10]" for his theories. Watson is a faithful[11] friend and he does provide[12] support[13] to Holmes.

Helen Stoner

I asked Sherlock Holmes for his help because I am afraid for my life.
My sister died under very mysterious[14] circumstances[15], and now I fear I am next.

James Ryder

I'm really not such a bad man. The stone was just so big and beautiful. I couldn't help[16] taking it. But I lost the stone! I guess I'm not a very good criminal[17].

The King of Bohemia

Being a king isn't always good, you know. Sometimes you have to marry someone you don't love. My current[18] concern[19] is that Irene Adler, my ex-girlfriend, would try to stop me from[20] marrying the royal lady. Hopefully Sherlock Holmes, can help me.

---

1. **detective(s)** [dɪˋtektɪv(z)] (n.) 偵探
2. **figure out** 算出；想出
3. **observation** [ˌɑ:bzərˋveɪʃən] (n.) 觀察
4. **deduction** [dɪˋdʌkʃən] (n.) 推論；演繹（法）
5. **incredible** [ɪnˋkredəbl] (a.) 難以置信的；驚人的
6. **mystery** [ˋmɪstri] (n.) 神祕之事；謎
7. **unsolvable** [ʌnˋsɑ:lvəbl] (a.) 無法解決的
8. **in trouble** 處於困難之中
9. **up to** 忙於某事
10. **sounding board** 被用作試探意見之人
11. **faithful** [ˋfeɪθfəl] (a.) 忠實的
12. **provide** [prəˋvaɪd] (v.) 提供
13. **support** [səˋpɔ:rt] (n.) 支持
14. **mysterious** [mɪˋstɪriəs] (a.) 神祕的；不可思議的
15. **circumstance(s)** [ˋsɜ:rkəmstæns(ɪz)] (n.) 情況；環境
16. **cannot help** 忍不住做了某事（後接動名詞）
17. **criminal** [ˋkrɪmɪnl] (n.) 罪犯
18. **current** [ˋkɜ:rənt] (a.) 現時的；當前的
19. **concern** [kənˋsɜ:rn] (n.) 關心的事；擔心；掛念
20. **stop A from** 阻止 A 做某事（後接動名詞）

13

The Adventure of the Speckled Band

斑繩記

Chapter One

Helen Stoner

I awoke[1] very early one morning in April 1883. Sherlock Holmes and I were living together. I looked at the clock and saw that it was only seven.

Usually Holmes liked to sleep in late, but he was already dressed[2], hovering[3] over me. I looked up at him in surprise[4].

"What is it, Holmes?" I asked. "Is there a fire?"

"No, there is a woman here. I think it is a case[5]. I know you will want to hear everything from the beginning[6], Watson," he said.

1. **awake** [əˋweɪk] (v.) 醒來 (awake-awoke-awoken)
2. **dressed** [drest] (a.) 穿好衣服的；打扮好的
3. **hover** [ˋhʌvər] (v.) 徘徊；停留
4. **in surprise** 驚訝地
5. **case** [keɪs] (n.) 案件
6. **from the beginning** 從頭開始
7. **downstairs** [daʊnˋsterz] (adv.) 往樓下
8. **sitting room** 起居室
9. **immediately** [ɪˋmiːdɪətli] (adv.) 立即；即刻；馬上

I quickly got dressed and went downstairs[7] with Holmes. We saw a lady in the sitting room[8]. She immediately[9] stood up when we entered the room. She was dressed in black[10] and her expression[11] was very grave[12].

"Good morning! I am Sherlock Holmes and this is Dr. Watson. He is my dear friend and associate[13]," Holmes said. "We would like to hear everything."

We all sat down.

10. **dressed in black**
　　穿著黑色衣服
11. **expression** [ɪk`spreʃən] (n.)
　　表情；臉色
12. **grave** [greɪv] (a.) 嚴肅的
13. **associate** [ə`souʃiət] (n.)
　　夥伴；同事；朋友

"I am Helen Stoner. I am living with my stepfather[1], Dr. Grimesby Roylott," she explained[2]. "The Roylotts have lived at Stoke Moran for centuries[3], but now my stepfather is the last[4] living Roylott. The family was once very wealthy."

Holmes nodded[5]. "I know the name," said he.

Miss Stoner went on[6]. "However, because of a long line[7] of terrible men, the family fortune is all gone. There is only the little land and the two-hundred-year-old house left[8].

My stepfather knew that there was no money for him to live on. So he studied to become a doctor and then went to India. When my mother met Dr. Roylott there, my father had only been dead for one year. Julia, my twin-sister[9], and I were only two years old at that time."

1. **stepfather** [ˋstepfɑːðə(r)] (n.) 繼父；後父
2. **explain** [ɪkˋspleɪn] (v.) 解釋
3. **for centuries** 有幾百年之久
4. **last** [læst] (a.) 最後的；僅剩的
5. **nod** [nɑːd] (v.) 點頭
6. **go on** 繼續
7. **line** [laɪn] (n.) （等待順序的）行列
8. **left** [left] (a.) 遺留下來的
9. **twin-sister** [ˋtwɪnˋsɪstə(r)] (n.) 孿生姐妹
10. **pound** [paʊnd] (n.) 英鎊
11. **will** [wɪl] (n.) 遺囑
12. **take care of** 照顧

"Your mother had some money, perhaps?" asked Sherlock Holmes.

"Oh, yes. She had about one thousand pounds[10] per year. My mother changed her will[11] when they married. She left all her money to him, but she did say in her will that he must take care of[12] Julia and me."

"We eventually[1] returned to England but our mother died soon after[2]. We all went to live at Stoke Moran. We had enough money but Roylott changed after our mother died. She was killed in a railway[3] accident[4] eight years ago.

He is surly[5] and fights with anyone in our neighborhood[6]. Everyone is scared of[7] him because he is strong and crazy. The only people he talks to are some gypsies[8] who live on his land.

He keeps some wild animals, too. There is a cheetah[9] and a baboon[10] which he brought back from India. They run freely around the place.

You can imagine from what I say that my sister and I had a hard time[11]. Because everyone is afraid of my stepfather, no one will work for us. We have to do everything.

Sadly, Julia has already died. She was only thirty at the time of her death, but her hair was already going gray[12]. My hair is becoming gray too."

1. **eventually** [ɪ`ventʃuəli] (adv.) 最後
2. **soon after** 不久之後
3. **railway** [`reɪlweɪ] (n.) 〔主英〕鐵路;鐵道
4. **accident** [`æksɪdənt] (n.) 意外事故
5. **surly** [`sɜːrli] (a.) 脾氣壞的;乖戾的
6. **neighborhood** [`neɪbərhʊd] (n.) 鄰近地區
7. **be scared of** 害怕（某人或某事）
8. **gypsy** [`dʒɪpsi] (n.) 吉普賽人
9. **cheetah** [`tʃiːtə] (n.) 印度豹
10. **baboon** [bæ`buːn] (n.) 狒狒
11. **have a hard time** 過苦日子
12. **go gray** 頭髮變灰白色

"Your sister is dead, then?"

"She died two years ago. This is why I have come to see you. We very rarely[1] left Stoke Moran but we sometimes visited our aunt. On one of those visits, Julia met a man. She fell in love[2] and they were planning to get married[3]. Our stepfather never verbally[4] opposed[5] the wedding[6] but in about ten days, Julia was dead."

Holmes had been leaning back[7] in his chair, quietly with his eyes closed as she told her story. He now sat up[8] quickly and said, "Tell us every tiny[9] detail[10]."

1. **rarely** [ˋrerli] (adv.)
   很少;難得
2. **fall in love** 談戀愛
3. **get married** 結婚
4. **verbally** [ˋvɜːrbəli] (adv.)
   言詞上;口頭地
5. **oppose** [əˋpouz] (v.)
   反對;反抗
6. **wedding** [ˋwedɪŋ] (n.)
   結婚典禮
7. **lean back** 向後傾
8. **sit up** 坐直身子
9. **tiny** [ˋtaɪni] (a.) 微小的
10. **detail** [ˋdiːteɪl] (n.) 細節
11. **wing** [wɪŋ] (n.)
    〔建〕側廳;廂房
12. **connect** [kəˋnekt] (v.)
    連接;連結
13. **hall** [hɔːl] (n.) 門廳;走廊
14. **cigar** [sɪˋgɑː(r)] (n.) 雪茄菸
15. **tend to** 有……的傾向

"I can tell you everything. It is as clear in my mind as if it happened just last night. As I have said, our house is very old and we live in only one wing[11] of it. Dr. Roylott's bedroom is the first, Julia's is the second and mine is the third. There are no doors connecting[12] the rooms. They just open out into the same long hall[13]. That night, Dr. Roylott went to his room early. We knew he hadn't gone to sleep because Julia could smell his cigars[14]. He tended to[15] smoke cigars in his room."

One Point Lesson

♦ Holmes had been leaning back in his chair, quietly **with his eyes closed** as she told her story.
她在說她的故事時，福爾摩斯一直靠著椅背，閉眼靜靜聽著。

---

with＋A 的身體器官 ＋ 過去分詞：A 以某身體器官活動狀態做某事

e.g. She was listening to me **with her arms crossed**.
她雙臂交叉聽我說話。

23

"Julia always hated that smell. So she came to my room. We talked for quite a while[1], mainly[2] about her wedding. At about 11 p.m., she got up to go back to her room. Just as she was leaving, she asked, 'Do you ever hear any whistling[3] in the early hours of the morning?'

I told her that I had never heard anything. Then she asked me if I whistled in my sleep. I told her, 'No. I don't think so. Why do you ask me that?'

She said that she always heard a whistle in the quiet of[4] the night at about three in the morning. She was a light sleeper[5] and any noise woke her up.

She said that she had tried to find out[6] where the noise[7] was coming from. She didn't know whether it was coming from[8] the room next door or from outside. I told her that maybe it was coming from the gypsies. She agreed and left to return to her room. I heard her enter her room and lock[9] the door."

1. **quite a while** 一陣子
2. **mainly** [`meɪnli] (adv.) 主要地；大部分地
3. **whistling** [`wɪslɪŋ] (n.) 口哨聲
4. **in the quiet of** 在安靜的狀態中
5. **light sleeper** [`laɪtsli:pə(r)] (n.) 容易醒來的人
6. **find out** 找出
7. **noise** [nɔɪz] (n.) 聲響；噪音
8. **come from** 來自於
9. **lock** [lɑːk] (v.) 鎖；鎖上

25

"Did you always lock your rooms at night?" Holmes asked.

"Yes, every night. We were worried about[1] the cheetah and the baboon," she replied.

"Yes, of course you would have been. Please go on with your story."

"That night, I tossed and turned[2] all night. I did not sleep a wink[3]. We were twins and people say that twins can sense[4] things about each other. I had a terrible feeling of disaster[5]. It was a very windy night and the rain pounded[6] against the windows. Then I heard a blood-curdling[7] scream[8]. I knew it was my sister's voice.

I sprang[9] from my bed. As I ran to my sister's room, I heard a whistling sound and then a clanging[10] sound as if a mass of[11] metal[12] had fallen. She opened her door slowly.

1. **be worried about**
   擔心……；焦慮……
2. **toss and turn** 翻來覆去
3. **not sleep a wink**
   〔口〕沒闔一下眼
4. **sense** [sens] (v.)
   感覺到；意識到
5. **disaster** [dɪˋzæstə(r)]
   (n.) 災難

6. **pound** [paʊnd]
   (v.)（猛烈）敲打
7. **blood-curdling**
   [ˋblʌdkɜːrdlɪŋ] (a.)
   令人毛骨悚然的
8. **scream** [skriːm] (n.) 尖叫
9. **spring** [sprɪŋ] (v.) 彈起
10. **clang** [klæŋ] (v.) 發鏗鏘聲
11. **a mass of** 眾多；大量

By the light of the corridor[13] lamp, her face was white with terror[14]. I threw my arms around her, but at the moment she fell to the floor.

Her last words were, "It was the band[15]! The speckled[16] band!"

She died instantly[17].

12. **metal** [ˋmetl] (n.) 金屬
13. **corridor** [ˋkɔːrɪdɔː(r)] (n.) 走廊
14. **with terror** 感到恐懼
15. **band** [bænd] (n.) 帶；細繩
16. **speckled** [ˋspekəld] (a.) 有斑點的
17. **instantly** [ˋɪnstəntli] (adv.) 立即地；即刻地

🎧7 "You are absolutely[1] sure you heard a whistle and a clanging sound?" Holmes asked Helen.

"Oh yes! I will never forget that."

"Was your sister wearing her nightdress[2]?"

"Yes, and we found a match box[3] in her hand."

"What did the police say about the case?"

"They investigated[4] it thoroughly[5] but they never found the cause[6] of her death. The windows were closed with bars[7] on them, the walls and floor are thick and her door was locked. Nobody could have entered the room," said Miss Stoner.

---

1. **absolutely** [ˋæbsəluːtli] (adv.) 絕對地；完全地
2. **nightdress** [ˋnaɪtdrɛs] (n.) 女睡袍
3. **match box** 火柴盒

4. **investigate** [ɪnˋvɛstɪgeɪt] (v.) 調查
5. **thoroughly** [ˋθɜːrəli] (adv.) 徹底地；認真仔細地
6. **cause** [kɔːz] (n.) 起因

The Adventure of the Speckled Band

Holmes listened to this intently[8], and he had a very serious[9] expression on his face.

"I don't like the sound of this. Please finish your story Miss Stoner," he told her.

"Well, it's been two years since my sister's death. I have been lonelier[10] than ever and missed[11] her very much. But I recently met a man, and he asked me to marry him. His name is Percy Armitage. We want to get married in the spring. My stepfather has said nothing about my marriage."

7. **bar** [bɑːr] (n.) 閂；橫槓
8. **intently** [ɪnˈtentli] (adv.) 專心地；專注地
9. **serious** [ˈsɪriəs] (a.) 嚴肅的
10. **lonely** [ˈlounli] (a.) 孤獨的；寂寞的
11. **miss** [mɪs] (v.) 想念；思念

🎧 8

"But two days ago he told me to move into Julia's room to make repairs¹ in mine. Last night, while in Julia's room, I heard the sound of a low whistle. It was the same sound Julia had talked about — on the night she had died! I was terrified² and I immediately lit³ a candle. I couldn't see anything.

1. **make repairs** 做整修
2. **terrified** [ˈtɛrɪfaɪd] (a.) 感到極度恐懼的
3. **light** [laɪt] (v.) 點（火）
4. **needless to say** 不用說
5. **daybreak** [ˈdeɪbreɪk] (n.) 破曉；黎明
6. **get into** 進入
7. **without** 沒有（做某事）（後接動名詞）
8. **be away** 不在（某處）
9. **inform** [ɪnˈfɔːrm] (v.) 告知
10. **advise** [ədˈvaɪz] (v.) 建議

Needless to say[4], I couldn't sleep. As soon as daybreak[5] came, I quickly dressed and came here."

Holmes sat in his chair thinking. After a while, he said, "This is very serious. We will come to Stoke Moran this afternoon. How can we get into[6] the house without[7] the doctor knowing?"

"He will be away[8] all day today," she informed[9] them.

"Good, we will arrive this afternoon. I advise[10] that you return now and wait for us."

Miss Stoner immediately left us.

One Point Lesson

- I **advise** that you **(should)** return now and wait for us. 我建議你（應該）現在回去等我們。

【句型】advise, recommend that sb + (should) + 原型動詞片語：建議某人做某事

- He **recommended** that the young girl **(should)** stay home at nights.
他建議那名女孩每晚（應該）留在家中。

Was Sherlock Holmes real?

S ir Conan Arthur Doyle included so many details about Holmes in his stories that he seems like a real person, and some people believe he actually did exist!

If you could meet Holmes, you would see a tall, thin man, about 185 centimeters in height[1]. Holmes had a long, narrow nose that was hooked[2]. His forehead was usually locked in a frown[3] as he was constantly[4] analyzing[5] information.

The Statue of Sherlock Holmes

Holmes lived in an apartment at 221b Baker Street, London, England, his native country. He studied for two years at a medical[6] university.

While at St. Bart's Hospital, he was introduced to Dr. John Watson. Watson would later become Holmes' best friend and biographer[7]. They lived together until Watson got married. Holmes never married and in fact seemed to dislike women.

Mrs. Hudson, Holmes' faithful landlady[8], often scolded[9] Holmes for being messy[10], as he left piles of papers everywhere. He also made messes[11] when he performed chemistry[12] experiments[13]. In addition to these, Holmes spent his free time playing the violin, writing scientific articles[14] about chemistry, beekeeping[15] or tobacco.

Those who think Holmes was a real person assume[16] he retired[17] to the English countryside, where he pursued[18] his hobby of beekeeping!

1. **height** [haɪt] (n.) 高度
2. **hooked** [hʊkt] (a.) 鉤狀的
3. **frown** [fraʊn] (n.) 皺眉；蹙額
4. **constantly** [`kɑːntstəntli] (adv.) 不斷地；時常地
5. **analyze** [`ænəlaɪz] (v.) 分析
6. **medical** [`medɪkl] (a.) 醫學的；醫療的
7. **biographer** [baɪ`ɑːgrəfə(r)] (n.) 傳記作者
8. **landlady** [`lænd͵leɪdi] (n.) 女房東
9. **scold** [skoʊld] (v.) 責罵；嘮嘮叨叨地責備

10. **messy** [`mesi] (a.) 混亂的；骯髒的
11. **mess** [mes] (n.) 混亂
12. **chemistry** [`kemɪstri] (n.) 化學
13. **experiment** [ɪk`sperɪmənt] (n.) 實驗
14. **article** [`ɑːrtɪkl] (n.) 文章
15. **beekeeping** [`biːkiːpɪŋ] (n.) 養蜂
16. **assume** [ə`suːm] (v.) 猜想；以為
17. **retire** [rɪ`taɪə(r)] (v.) 退隱
18. **pursue** [pər`suː] (v.) 進行；從事

Chapter Two

An Urgent[1] Matter[2]

"**W**hat do you think of it all, Watson?" Holmes asked.

"It seems to me to be a most dark business[3]," I said.

"Dark enough. This is a very urgent case, Watson. The most important clue[4] is Julia's last words, 'the speckled band.' It could have been the gypsies whistling and clanging. But I don't think so. Let's eat breakfast. I will go into town for something, and then we will leave."

Holmes came back at about one o'clock. He was carrying a sheet of[5] blue paper. It was the will[6] of Helen and Julia's mother.

"Mrs. Stoner left ten thousand pounds. But the girls are supposed to[7] receive two thousand and five hundred pounds each when they marry. If they don't marry, or both die first, the doctor is to get all of the money. There is a motive[8] right there. Let's go Watson and bring your gun."

Holmes and I left to catch a train. We had to hire[9] a horse and cart[10] to get to[11] Stoke Moran.

1. **urgent** [ˋɜːrdʒənt] (a.)
   緊急的
2. **matter** [ˋmætə(r)] (n.) 事件
3. **dark business** 邪惡的事
4. **clue** [kluː] (n.) 線索
5. **a sheet of**
   （紙等的）一張
6. **will** [wɪl] (n.) 遺囑

7. **be supposed to** 應該
8. **motive** [ˋmoʊtɪv] (n.) 動機
9. **hire** [ˋhaɪə(r)] (v.) 租；租借
10. **cart** [kɑːrt] (n.)
    （馬、牛等拉的）二輪
    （或四輪）運貨車
11. **get to** 抵達

As soon as we arrived, Helen came out.

She was fretting[1] and said, "I have been waiting for you."

"Don't worry, Miss Stoner. We will get to the bottom[2] of this," Holmes assured[3] her. "Please show me your bedrooms."

Helen showed us where the bedrooms were. Then Holmes walked along the outside of the house. He looked at the window.

"First, go into your room and lock it," said Holmes to Helen.

After she locked her room, Holmes tried to open it but was unsuccessful[4]. He also tried to get in through the windows but, again, was unsuccessful.

We then went into Julia's room. It was a small room with a low ceiling[5]. Holmes sat in a chair and looked around. He did not speak for a while.

1. **fret** [fret] (v.)
   苦惱；煩躁；發愁
2. **get to the bottom**
   弄清⋯⋯的真相
3. **assure** [əˋʃur] (v.)
   向⋯⋯保證；使放心
4. **unsuccessful**
   [ˏʌnsəkˋsɛsfl] (a.) 失敗的

Then he said, "There is a bell-pull[6]!"

There was a long rope dangling[7] from the ceiling.

"Where does the bell ring[8]?" he asked her.

"Downstairs. It is supposed to be used to call the servants[9] but as we don't have any, we never use it."

5. **ceiling** [ˋsiːlɪŋ] (n.) 天花板
6. **bell-pull** [ˋbɛlpʊl] (n.) 鐘繩
7. **dangle** [ˋdæŋgəl] (v.) 懸吊

8. **ring** [rɪŋ] (v.) （鐘或鈴等）鳴；響 (ring-rang-rung)
9. **servant** [ˋsɜːrvənt] (n.) 僕人

"This bell-pull looks newer than the other things." said Holmes.

"Yes, my stepfather put it in only a couple of years ago," replied Helen.

Holmes went over and pulled on[1] the rope.

"It doesn't do anything. Look! It's attached to[2] that air vent[3]. Why is there an air vent there? An air vent should go outside but this one leads to[4] the next room. Let's look more closely[5]."

We all went into the doctor's room. It was a strange room. There were only three things: a bed, a wooden chair and an iron safe[6].

"What is in the safe?" Holmes asked the woman.

"My stepfather's documents[7]."

"Does your stepfather keep[8] a cat?"

Holmes was pointing to[9] a dish on the floor with milk in it.

"There are only the cheetah and the baboon. That milk would not be enough for a cheetah."

Holmes looked around some more. He picked up[10] a small dog leash[11]. There was a small loop[12] at the end of it.

Suddenly, Holmes's face became even more serious. He looked extremely[13] worried. We went outside and Holmes walked around for quite some time.

1. **pull on** 用力拉
2. **be attached to** 附屬於
3. **air vent** 通風孔；排氣孔
4. **lead to** 通到（某處）
5. **closely** [`kloʊsli] (adv.) 嚴密地；仔細地
6. **safe** [seɪf] (n.) 保險箱
7. **document** [`dɑːkjumənt] (n.) 文件
8. **keep** [kiːp] (v.) 飼養
9. **point to** 指向
10. **pick up** 拾起
11. **leash** [liːʃ] (n.) （栓狗用的）皮帶；鏈條
12. **loop** [luːp] (n.) （線或鐵絲等繞成的）圈；環
13. **extremely** [ɪk`striːmli] (adv.) 極端地；極其；非常

"This is an extremely serious situation. You must do everything I tell you. It is vital[1]."

Miss Stoner nodded her head.

"We are going to stay at the inn[2] over there tonight," said Holmes, pointing at an inn across the street.

"Tonight, you must stay in your sister's room just as you did last night. When your stepfather goes to bed, I want you to light a candle and blow it out[3] after a few moments. That will be a signal[4] for us. Then, go to your room and wait for us. We will enter the house and stay in Julia's room."

"You know how my sister died, don't you? Please tell me," Miss Stoner begged[5].

"I am not completely[6] sure yet. We have to wait until tonight. The doctor cannot see us, so we must go."

We left the house and went to the inn to wait. We had a room from which we could see Stoke Moran. At about seven in the evening, Dr. Roylott arrived home. We could hear him yelling at[7] the boy who opened the gate.

At about nine o'clock, all of the lights went out[8]. We waited for about two more hours until we saw a flash of[9] light in the window.

"That is our signal. Let's go," said Holmes.

1. **vital** [`vaɪtl] (a.) 生死攸關的
2. **inn** [ɪn] (n.) 小旅館；客棧
3. **blow out** 吹熄
   (blow-blew-blown)
4. **signal** [`sɪgnəl] (n.)
   信號；暗號
5. **beg** [bɛg] (v.) 請求；懇求
   (beg-begged-begged)
6. **completely** [kəm`pliːtli]
   (adv.) 完全地；徹底地
7. **yell at** 對……叫喊
8. **go out** 熄滅
9. **a flash of** 一道閃光

13

We quickly made our way to[1] the old house.
A cold wind blew in our faces. We climbed in
through Julia's window which Helen had left[2]
open. We had to be very quiet so as not to[3] wake
the doctor. We did not dare[4] have a light, either.
Roylott might see it through the air vent.

1. **make one's way to** 向前走
2. **leave** [liːv] (v.)
   使處於某種狀態
3. **so as not to** 以免
4. **dare** [der] (v.) 敢；膽敢
5. **whisper** [ˈwɪspə(r)] (v.)
   低語；耳語；私語
6. **lose one's life** 喪失生命
7. **reassure oneself**
   使自己放心
8. **dreadful** [ˈdredfəl] (a.)
   可怕的；令人恐懼的
9. **painful** [ˈpeɪnfəl] (a.)
   痛苦的

"Neither of us must fall asleep," whispered[5] Holmes. "We may lose our lives[6] if we do."

I put my hand on my gun to help reassure myself[7]. How could I forget that dreadful[8] night? The waiting was painful[9]. It was one of the longest nights of my life. One hour passed. Then, two. Then, three.

At three o'clock, we could see a faint[10] light through the air vent. Then, there was a hissing sound[11]. Holmes, being frightened[12], lit a match and ran to the wall. He began to hit it violently[13].

"Did you see that, Watson? Did you see it?" he asked me. But I couldn't see anything. When Holmes lit the match, I had heard a low whistle. But I could not see what Holmes had hit. I could, however, see that his face was deadly[14] pale[15] and filled with horror[16].

10. **faint** [feɪnt] (a.) 微弱的
11. **hissing sound** 嘶嘶聲
12. **frightened** [ˋfraɪtnd] (a.) 受驚的；〔口〕害怕的
13. **violently** [ˋvaɪələntli] (adv.) 激烈地；猛烈地
14. **deadly** [ˋdedli] (adv.) 死一般地
15. **pale** [peɪl] (a.) 蒼白的
16. **horror** [ˋhɔːrə(r)] (n.) 恐懼

We stood very still[1] and a short time later, we heard a terrible scream. The sound made my blood run cold[2]. They say that people heard the cry all the way[3] down in the village. I still have nightmares[4] thinking about it.

"What was that scream?" I asked.

"It means this case is all over now," Holmes informed me. "Come with me to the doctor's room. And bring your gun."

A strange sight[5] met my eyes. We noticed[6] that the safe was now open. The doctor was sitting in the wooden chair that we had seen earlier that day. The small dog leash was in his lap[7].

He was dead and his eyes were looking toward the ceiling. Wrapped around[8] his head, we could see a yellow creature[9] with brown spots[10].

---

1. **stand still** 站著不動
2. **run cold (one's blood . . .)** 感到害怕；恐懼
3. **all the way** 整個途中
4. **nightmare** [`naɪtmer] (n.) 夢魘；惡夢
5. **sight** [saɪt] (n.) 景色；景象
6. **notice** [`noutɪs] (v.) 注意
7. **lap** [læp] (n.) 大腿部
8. **wrap around** 纏繞；盤繞
9. **creature** [`kriːtʃə(r)] (n.) 生物

"That is the speckled band," declared[11] Holmes. The band began to move. It lifted[12] its head. It was a snake!

"It is a swamp[13] adder[14] from India. It is the most dangerous snake in India," said Holmes. "Let's put it back[15] into the cage[16]."

Holmes picked up the leash. He looped[17] it around the snake's head. He carried the snake to the safe and closed the door.

10. **spot** [spɑːt] (n.) 斑點；斑塊
11. **declare** [dɪˋkler] (v.) 宣佈
12. **lift** [lɪft] (v.) 舉起
13. **swamp** [swɑːmp] (n.) 沼澤
14. **adder** [ˋædə(r)] (n.) 奎蛇
15. **put back** 把……放回原處
16. **cage** [keɪdʒ] (n.) 籠子
17. **loop** [luːp] (v.) 用環扣住（或套住）

The next day, the police stated[1] that Dr. Roylott had died from playing with a dangerous animal.

"I knew something was strange when I saw the bell-pull connected to the air vent. Dr. Roylott liked exotic[2] animals, so I thought he might have a snake too. He trained[3] the snake to crawl[4] through the vent and go down the rope. Whenever he whistled, the snake returned. The dish of milk was for the snake.

The doctor successfully killed Julia with the snake, so I guess he was going to try the same trick[5] with Helen. As soon as[6] I heard the hissing sound, I hit it. I made the snake go back the way it came," Holmes explained.

"Yes, and by hitting it, you made it angry. It went back and bit[7] the doctor," I said.

"Really, I guess I am the one who caused[8] the doctor to die. I am glad it was him and not Helen, you or I."

1. **state** [steɪt] (v.) 說明
2. **exotic** [ɪgˋzɑːtɪk] (a.) 外來的；外國產的
3. **train** [treɪn] (v.) 訓練
4. **crawl** [krɔːl] (v.) 爬；爬行
5. **try a trick with** 嘗試戲弄某人
6. **as soon as** 一⋯⋯就⋯⋯
7. **bite** [baɪt] (v.) 咬 (bite-bit-bitten)
8. **cause** [kɔːz] (v.) 導致；使發生

◉ Really, I guess I am the one **who** caused the
doctor to die. 說真的，我猜我才是殺死醫生的兇手

關係代名詞 who：代替先前出現的人（先行詞），用來引
導關係子句（作為形容詞子句），來修飾它所替代的詞。
who 及 which（代表物）在句中當主詞及受詞時均可以
that 替代。

e.g. (1) I know a boy.　　(2) The boy passed the test.
　→ I know the boy **who** passed the test.
　　我知道那名通過考試的男孩。

A Match.

1 fret • • **a** A loud sound made with metal objects.

2 gypsies • • **b** To greatly worry about something.

3 urgent • • **c** To hang a rope or string from a high place.

4 clang • • **d** To be extremely important.

5 safe • • **e** People who travel about with no home.

6 dangle • • **f** An object used to keep documents secure.

B Fill in the blanks with the antonyms of the words underlined.

1 Holmes usually got up <u>very early</u> in the morning.

→ _____

2 The Roylott family had <u>earned</u> a lot of money.

→ _____

3 Everyone in the neighborhood <u>gets</u> along well with Dr. Roylott. → _____

4 The sisters lived on <u>different floors</u> of the house.

→ _____

5 Helen has <u>continued to live in her own room</u>.

→ _____

C Choose the correct answer.

❶ What would happen if the two sisters didn't marry?

(a) They would receive two hundred and fifty pounds.

(b) Dr. Roylott would continue to receive ten thousand pounds.

(c) They would be forced to marry.

❷ What did Holmes and Watson wait for at the inn?

(a) A sign that the stepfather was asleep.

(b) A sign to come and meet the stepfather.

(c) A sign to catch the gypsies.

❸ Why did the snake bite Dr. Roylott?

(a) Because it was trained to do so.

(b) Because the snake didn't like people.

(c) Because it had become angry.

D Fill in the blanks with simple past tense or present tense.

Holmes had **❶** _____ (sit) in his chair, quietly listening to the woman as she **❷** _____ (tell) her story. He now **❸** _____ (sit up) quickly and said, "Tell us every tiny detail."

"I can tell you everything. It **❹** _____ (be) as clear in my mind as if it happened just last night. Our house is very old and we **❺** _____ (live) in only one wing of it. "

The Adventure of the Blue Carbuncle

藍寶石案

Chapter One

The Mysterious[1] Stone

It was a couple of[2] days after Christmas, and I decided to call in on[3] my good friend, Sherlock Holmes.

He was lying on his sofa, smoking his pipe and looking like he was very deep in thought[4].

I glanced[5] around the room and noticed a very dirty, black, torn[6] hat hanging[7] on the back of a chair. I also noticed a magnifying glass[8] on the chair. I assumed[9] that Holmes had been examining[10] it.

---

1. **mysterious** [mɪˋstɪrɪəs] (a.)
   神秘的；不可思議的
2. **a couple of** 幾個；數個
3. **call in on** 拜訪
4. **deep in thought** 陷入沉思

5. **glance** [ɡlæns] (v.)
   略看一下；一瞥
6. **torn** [tɔːrn] (a.) 扯破的
7. **hang** [hæŋ] (v.) 懸掛；吊著
   (hang-hung-hung)

The Adventure of the Blue Carbuncle

"You are busy," I said. "Perhaps I interrupt[11] you."

After some moments had passed, Holmes finally spoke.

"Not at all. The problem is simple and it is still interesting. You know the doorman, Peterson, don't you?" he asked. "He found that hat and brought it here. He also found it with a large, fat goose. He's cooking the goose now."

"The facts are these. Peterson went to a party on Christmas Eve which went on until very late the next morning. When Peterson was walking home at about 4 a.m., he saw a man walking in front of him. He was a tall man. He was carrying the goose and he was also wearing that hat."

8. **magnifying glass** 放大鏡
9. **assume** [ə`suːm] (v.)
   以為；假定為

10. **examine** [ɪg`zæmɪn] (v.)
    檢查；細查
11. **interrupt** [ˌɪntə`rʌpt] (v.)
    打擾

53

17

"The tall man walked along a little further[1] when a group of men suddenly appeared and attacked him. He fought back[2] with his stick[3], but ended up[4] breaking a window behind him. The sound of the breaking glass made him drop the goose and run. He also left his hat behind[5], which had been knocked off[6] during the fight. The gang of thieves ran off[7] too. Peterson was left to pick up the hat and the goose."

"Peterson went in search of[8] the owner[9], didn't he?" I asked.

"Well, that is the problem. We know who the owner is. There was a tag[10] tied to[11] the goose with the owner's name, 'For Mrs. Henry Baker." Inside the hat are the initials[12] H. B. I am sure the owner of the hat must be Mr. Henry Baker, but there are so many Henry Bakers in London. Peterson brought me the hat, but the goose had to be cooked. It would just be ruined[13] otherwise[14]."

1. **further** [ˋfɜːrðə(r)] (adv.) 更遠地；較遠地
2. **fight back**〔英〕回擊
3. **stick** [stɪk] (n.) 棍；棒
4. **end up** 結果……（後接動名詞）
5. **leave behind** 留下
6. **knock off** 撞倒；打掉
7. **run off** 逃跑
8. **in search of** 尋找
9. **owner** [ˋoʊnə(r)] (n.) 擁有者
10. **tag** [tæg] (n.) 牌子；標籤
11. **tied to** 繫在某物上
12. **initial** [ɪˋnɪʃəl] (n.) 名字的首字母
13. **ruin** [ˋruːɪn] (v.) 毀壞

Suddenly, Peterson came running into the room. He was out of breath[15], sputtering[16], "The goose! The goose! My wife found this inside."

In his hand was a beautiful blue stone. It was about the size of a bean. But it was so pure[17] and bright that it twinkled[18] like a star.

"My Goodness[19]! Peterson! Do you know what you are holding?" Holmes asked.

"Is it the Countess[21] of Morcar's blue carbuncle[21]?" I asked.

---

14. **otherwise** [ˋʌðɚwaɪz] (adv.) 用別的方式地
15. **out of breath** 喘不過氣來
16. **sputter** [ˋspʌtə(r)] (v.) 結結巴巴地說話
17. **pure** [pjʊr] (a.) 純的；清亮的
18. **twinkle** [ˋtwɪŋkl] (v.) 閃耀
19. **my goodness!** 我的天哪！
20. **countess** [ˋkaʊntəs] (n.) 伯爵夫人
21. **carbuncle** [ˋkɑːrbʌŋkl] (n.) 〔礦〕紅玉

"I've been reading so much about it in the newspapers. There's a large reward[1] of one thousand pounds for its return. I read that it was stolen from the Countess's room at the Hotel Cosmopolitan[2]. Didn't the police arrest[3] someone for the theft? If I remember correctly, his name is John Horner, a plumber[4]. In fact, I think I have the story right here," said I.

Holmes took the newspaper and started to read the article[5] aloud:

---

1. **reward** [rɪˋwɔːrd] (n.) 酬金
2. **cosmopolitan** [ˌkɑːzməˋpɑːlɪtən] (a.) 世界性的（在此為旅館名）
3. **arrest** [əˋrest] (v.) 逮捕
4. **plumber** [ˋplʌmə(r)] (n.) 水電工
5. **article** [ˋɑːrtɪkəl] (n.) 文章
6. **robbery** [ˋrɑːbəri] (n.) 搶劫
7. **allegedly** [əˋledʒɪdli] (adv.) 據宣稱
8. **employee** [ˌɪmˋplɔɪiː] (n.) 受雇者；雇員
9. **guilt** [gɪlt] (n.) 犯罪；過失
10. **leaky** [ˋliːki] (a.) 漏水的
11. **perform** [pərˋfɔːrm] (v.) 履行；執行

Jewel Robbery[6] at Hotel Cosmopolitan

John Horner, a local plumber, was arrested for theft at the Hotel Cosmopolitan today. According to the police, he allegedly[7] stole the jewel known as the blue carbuncle from the jewel case of the Countess of Morcar.

He was arrested after information provided by James Ryder, a hotel employee[8], pointed to Horner's guilt[9]. According to Ryder, Horner was sent to the Countess's room to fix a leaky[10] pipe. For a short period of time, Horner was left alone in the room while Ryder was called to perform[11] other duties.

On Ryder's return, Horner had left the room and the Countess's dresser had been forced open. The Countess's jewel box was on the table but it was empty. In a police statement[12], Horner had resisted[13] arrest claiming[14] that he was innocent[15]. However, Horner, already being a convicted[16] thief, is the most likely suspect[17]. He will remain in jail[18] until his trial[19].

12. **statement** [ˈsteɪtmənt] (n.) 〔律〕供述
13. **resist** [rɪˈzɪst] (v.) 反抗
14. **claim** [kleɪm] (v.) 聲稱
15. **innocent** [ˈɪnəsnt] (a.) 無罪的；清白的
16. **convicted** [kənˈvɪktɪd] (a.) 判決有罪的
17. **suspect** [ˈsʌspekt] (n.) 嫌疑犯
18. **jail** [dʒeɪl] (n.) 監獄
19. **trial** [traɪəl] (n.) 審判

Holmes finished reading the newspaper and threw it down on the table.

"It just shows that the police don't know very much, doesn't it?" he exclaimed[1]. "We know that he may be innocent. But Watson! One thing we must first find out is how the stone got into the bird. There are a few things we already know. This is the stone. The stone was inside the goose which came from Henry Baker. Our first task[2] is to find Henry Baker. Get me a pencil and paper."

Holmes wrote the following[3]:

> *One large fat goose and a black felt hat[4] belonging to[5] a Mr. Henry Baker found at the corner of Goodge Street. The owner may receive his possessions[6] at 221B Baker Street at 6:30 this evening.*

"There. That's clear." Holmes handed[7] the paper to Peterson.

"Here, Mr. Peterson! I would like you to put this message into all of the evening newspapers. *The Globe. The Star. The Evening News. The Herald.* All of them. And if there are any others, put the message in them as well."

"Yes, sir. I will do it immediately," replied[8] Peterson.

1. **exclaim** [ɪk`skleɪm] (v.)
   大聲說出；呼喊著說出
2. **task** [tæsk] (n.) 任務；工作
3. **following** [`fɑːloʊɪŋ] (n.)
   下列事物（或人員）
4. **felt hat** 一種男式軟呢帽
5. **belong to** 屬於
6. **possession(s)** [pə`zeʃn(z)]
   (n.) 所有物；財產
7. **hand to** 面交；給；傳遞
8. **reply** [rɪ`plaɪ] (v.)
   回答；答覆

"What will we do with the stone?" asked I.

"We will keep it here for now," Holmes informed us. "Peterson! On your way back home[1], buy another goose like the one that your family is eating now. We will need another bird to give back to Mr. Henry Baker."

Peterson left to attend to[2] his errands[3]. Holmes examined the stone for a while.

"It's quite spectacular[4], isn't it? It's what crimes[5] are made of. Look at it in the light! See how it shines[6] and sparkles[7]. It's a very valuable[8] stone I must say. This stone is only about twenty years old but it already has a sinister[9] history. There have been two murders[10], a suicide[11], and several robberies."

---

1. **on one's way back home** 在回家的路上
2. **attend to** 注意；致力於
3. **errand** [ˋɛrənd] (n.) 任務
4. **spectacular** [spɛkˋtækjələ(r)] (a.) 引人注目的；驚人的
5. **crime** [kraɪm] (n.) 罪；罪行
6. **shine** [ʃaɪn] (v.) 發光 (shine-shone-shone)
7. **sparkle** [ˋspɑːrkəl] (v.) 閃耀
8. **valuable** [ˋvæljuəblə] (a.) 值錢的
9. **sinister** [ˋsɪnɪstə(r)] (n.) 不幸的；災難性的
10. **murder** [ˋmɜːrdə(r)] (n.) 謀殺；凶殺
11. **suicide** [ˋsuːɪsaɪd] (n.) 自殺
12. **put away** 收好；儲存
13. **drop a line** 寫信

Holmes then put the stone away[12] in a safe place for keeping.

"I'll drop a line[13] to the Countess to say that we have it."

21

"Do you think that the plumber is guilty[1] or innocent?" I asked him.

"Well, it's very hard to say. Only time will give us the answers that we need."

"What about[2] Henry Baker? Do you think that he had something to do with[3] the theft?" I asked.

"My guess[4] is that he has no idea about it whatsoever[5]. But we will find out[6] tonight though[7] when he comes to claim[8] his goose and his hat. We can't do anything about this until then."

"Then, I should be going," I told Holmes. "I have many things I need to do. There are many sick people whom I need to visit. But I am very curious[9] about how this case proceeds[10]. I will return before 6:30 p.m. tonight if you do not mind," I said.

1. **guilty** [ˋgɪlti] (n.) 有罪的
2. **what about...?** （提出建議、詢問消息或徵求意見時使用）……如何？
3. **have something to do with** 跟……有關
4. **guess** [gɛs] (n.) 猜測；推測
5. **whatsoever** [wɑːtsouˋɛvə(r)] (a.) （在 no、any 連用的名詞之後）毫不（= whatever）
6. **find out** 找出；發現；查明
7. **though** [ðou] (adv.) （一般放在句尾）然而

"Of course not! I would like to have your thoughts on the matter too. Why don't you stay for dinner? We'll eat at seven."

I left Holmes there and I returned just before 6:30 that evening. I walked toward the house and I noticed that there was a tall man waiting outside. We both entered the house together.

Holmes welcomed us both in and said, "I trust[11] that you are Mr. Henry Baker."

The man said that he was and Holmes offered[12] him a chair by the fire.

8. **claim** [kleɪm] (v.)
   （根據權利）認領；索取
9. **curious** [`kjuriəs]
   (a.) 好奇的
10. **proceed** [prou`si:d] (v.)
    進行；開展
11. **trust** [trʌst] (v.) 〔書〕想
12. **offer** [`ɑːfə(r)] (v.) 提供

63

22

"You look like you are very cold. Ah, Watson, you have come just at the right time. Is this your hat?" Holmes asked the man.

"Yes, it is. And the bird?"

"Yes, the bird," Holmes said. "Uh-hum! Yes, the bird! Unfortunately[1] we had to eat it."

"You ate my bird!" the man exclaimed, looking quite upset[2].

"We had to. It would have been ruined if we didn't eat it then. We have another for you. It is about the same size. Surely[3] it will do to replace[4] the one we ate, won't it?"

"Yes, of course! It will be fine," said the man.

Holmes and I looked at each other. It was obvious[5] to us that the man knew nothing about the stone inside. He was just happy to have another bird to replace the one he had lost. Holmes then went and gave the man his hat and the bird.

"Just out of curiosity[6], where did you buy your goose from? It tasted very good and I'd like to get another one from where you got it," Holmes asked.

"I got it at the Alpha Inn. I go there almost every night. The owner started a goose club[7] and all of us in the club put in[8] a few pennies every week. At Christmas, everyone gets a goose. Thank you so much Mr. Holmes for the goose and my hat."

Mr. Baker said goodnight to us and left.

Holmes closed the door after him and said, "So much for Henry Baker."

1. **unfortunately**
   [ʌnˋfɔːrtʃənətli] (adv.)
   可惜地
2. **upset** [ʌpˋset] (a.)
   心煩的；苦惱的
3. **surely** [ˋʃʊrli] (adv.) 想必
4. **replace** [rɪˋpleɪs] (v.) 取代
5. **obvious** [ˋɑːbviəs] (a.)
   顯然的
6. **out of curiosity** 出於好奇
7. **club** [klʌb] (n.) 俱樂部
8. **put in** 存入；加進

221b Baker Street

The image of a man in a deerstalker[1] hat who is smoking a large pipe is easily recognized[2] by most people all over the world as Sherlock Holmes. He is perhaps the only character in recent literature who enjoys such instant[3] recognition[4]. Just as recognizable[5] is the address where Holmes lived in London: 221b Baker Street.

Doyle made up this address — it didn't exist. But it does now! So many tourists searched for this address in London that the British government finally rearranged[6] the street numbers so that a former lodging[7] house could be turned into[8] a Sherlock Holmes museum at this actual address! This museum faithfully recreates[9] Holmes' apartment from books and movies.

The sitting room where Holmes received new clients[10] and discussed cases with Watson looks just

1. **deerstalker** [ˋdɪrstɔːkə(r)] (n.) 獵鹿帽
2. **recognize** [ˋrekəgnaɪz] (v.) 認出；識別
3. **instant** [ˋɪnstənt] (a.) 立即的；即刻的
4. **recognition** [rekəgˋnɪʃən] (n.) 認出；識別

as it is described[11] in Doyle's stories. You can sit in one of the two armchairs[12] beside the fireplace and pretend that you are listening to Holmes explain some intricate[13] mystery. You can also see Holmes' famous hat and pipe, magnifying[14] glass, chemistry equipment[15], makeup[16] and wigs[17] for his many disguises[18] and so on.

Sherlock Holmes' Sitting Room

The Sherlock Holmes Museum

5. **recognizable** [ˋrekəgnaɪzəbəl] (a.) 可辨認的；可識別的

6. **rearrange** [riːəˋreɪndʒ] (v.) 重新排列

7. **lodging** [ˋlɑːdʒɪŋ] (n.) 寄宿；借宿

8. **turn into** 使變成

9. **recreate** [ˌriːkriˋeɪt] (v.) 改造；重新創造

10. **client** [ˋklaɪənt] (n.) 客戶

11. **describe** [dɪˋskraɪb] (v.) 描述

12. **armchair** [ˋɑːrmtʃer] (v.) 扶手椅

13. **intricate** [ˋɪntrɪkət] (n.) 錯綜複雜的；難理解的

14. **magnifying glass** 放大鏡

15. **equipment** [ɪˋkwɪpmənt] (n.) 設備

16. **makeup** [ˋmeɪkʌp] (n.) 化妝品

17. **wig** [wɪg] (n.) 假髮

18. **disguise** [dɪsˋgaɪz] (n.) 假扮；偽裝

· Chapter Two ·

The Goose Chase

🎧 23 It was now about 7 p.m. We had planned to have dinner at that time.

"Are you hungry, Watson?" Holmes asked me.

"Not really², " I replied.

"Let's eat later and follow this new clue³ while it is still hot," he said.

1. **chase** [tʃeɪs] (n.) 追尋
2. **not really** 並非如此
3. **clue** [kluː] (n.) 線索

4. **head** [hed] (v.)
　（向特定方向）出發
5. **bitterly** [ˋbɪtərli] (adv.)
　非常地

We got dressed and headed[4] outside. It was a bitterly[5] cold night. We put on[6] our overcoats[7] and wrapped up[8] our throats[9]. Outside the snow was falling heavily and the wind was blowing[10] hard. Our breath[11] looked like smoke. We quickly made our way to[12] the Alpha Inn. We went inside and ordered[13] two glasses of beer.

"I hope your beer tastes as good as your geese," Holmes said to the owner.

The owner looked surprised and said, "My geese?"

"Yes, I heard from Henry Baker. I believe that he is in your goose club."

"Oh! I see. They are not our geese. I bought them from a man who sells meat at Covent Garden[14]. Breckinridge is his name."

"Thank you very much sir," Holmes said as we put our coats back on[15].

6. **put on** 穿上
7. **overcoat** [`ouvərkout] (n.)
   外套；大衣
8. **wrap up** 穿暖和的衣服
9. **throat** [θrout] (n.) 喉嚨
10. **blow** [blou] (v.) 吹；刮
    (blow-blew-blown)

11. **breath** [brɛθ] (n.)
    呼吸；氣息 (v. breathe)
12. **make one's way to** 到達
13. **order** [`ɔːrdə(r)] (v.)
    點（菜或飲料）
14. **Covent Garden**
    倫敦柯芬園
15. **put A back on** 重新穿上 A

24

We went out again into the frosty[1] air.

"Now for Mr. Breckinridge," Holmes said as he buttoned[2] his coat.

Soon after, we found ourselves in[3] the Covent Garden market. We walked around until we saw a sign[4] with Breckinridge on it.

The owner was a horsey looking[5] man. He and a small boy were just closing up[6].

"Good evening. You wouldn't have any geese left tonight, would you?" Holmes asked the man.

"You can have five hundred in the morning," he replied.

"No, I want the same ones you sold to the Alpha Inn. They were fine birds. Where did you get them?"

1. **frosty** [ˋfrɔːsti] (a.)
   冷若冰霜的；嚴寒的
2. **button** [ˋbʌtn] (n.)
   扣上；扣住
3. **find oneself in**
   發現自己處於某種狀態
4. **sign** [saɪn] (n.)
   標誌；招牌；標牌
5. **horsey looking** 像馬臉的
6. **close up** 打烊

This question made the man very angry.

"I'm sick of[7] hearing about those birds. Everyone's been asking about them. I haven't heard anything else all day. You would think they were the only geese in the world. People are making such a fuss[8] about them," he snapped[9].

"Well, I don't know anything about the other people," said Holmes. He sounded[10] as if he did not care very much about it.

---

7. **be sick of** 討厭；厭倦
   （做某事）（後接動名詞）

8. **make a fuss**
   大驚小怪；小題大作

9. **snap** [snæp] (v.)
   厲聲說；怒氣沖沖地頂撞

10. **sound** [saʊnd] (v.) 聽起來

"But if you won't tell us where you got them from, I'll have to call off[1] my bet. I bet[2] five pounds that those geese were raised in the country," Holmes told the man.

"You will lose. Those geese were raised in town," Breckinridge said.

"No. I cannot believe that," Holmes said.

"I'll make a bet[3] with you," replied the man.

1. **call off** 取消
2. **bet** [bet] (v.) 賭注
3. **make a bet** 打賭
4. **open up** 開啟
5. **shilling** [ˈʃɪlɪŋ] (n.)
   先令（原英國貨幣單位）

6. **coin** [kɔɪn] (n.) 硬幣
7. **slam down**
   砰地放下（或放倒）
8. **storm** [stɔːrm] (v.)
   橫衝直撞；猛衝

Holmes laughed and said, "That will be an easy five pounds for me."

Breckinridge called to the boy, "Bring me my books!"

He opened up[4] his book.

"Look here. See this? It says December twenty-second, twenty-four geese at seven and a half shillings[5] each bought from Mrs. Oakshott, 117 Brixton Road, Number 249. Sold to the Alpha Inn at twelve shillings each. So, what do you think of that?"

Holmes pretended to be angry. He pulled a coin[6] from his pocket and slammed it down[7] on the table. He stormed[8] out of the market and I followed just behind.

One Point Lesson

◆ It **says** December twenty-second, twenty-four geese . . . 117 Brixton Road, Number 249.
第 249 頁上面寫「12 月 22 日，從布里克斯頓路 117 號的歐克夏太太那兒買來 24 隻鵝，每隻 7 先令半」。

---

say: 顯示；標明 (= read)

e.g. The clock **says** it's seven to ten.
時鐘顯示現在是九點五十三分。

26

When we had gotten completely out of the market, Holmes started laughing.

"It's so easy to get what you want. I noticed that the man likes to bet because he had a horse-racing[1] form[2] in his pocket. I knew he couldn't resist[3] a bet like that. Watson, we will have this case solved[4] very soon. Let's call it a night[5] and have dinner. We can visit Mrs. Oakshott tomorrow."

Just as Holmes finished speaking, we heard a loud noise back in the market. We could hear Breckinridge yelling[6]. We went inside and heard Breckinridge shout[7], "Get out of here[8]! I don't want to hear another word about those geese and I don't want to see you around here ever again!"

1. **horse-racing** 賽馬
2. **form** [fɔːrm] (n.) 表格
3. **resist** [rɪˋzɪst] (v.) 反抗
4. **solve** [sɑːlv] (v.) 解決
5. **let's call it a night.**
   今天就到此為止。
   (= Let's call it a day.)
6. **yell** [jɛl] (v.) 叫喊；吼叫
7. **shout** [ʃaʊt] (v.) 大聲叫
8. **get out of here!**
   離開這裡！
9. **after all** 畢竟
10. **come up** 走近；接近
11. **leap into the air** 嚇了一跳

"Hmm! Perhaps we don't need to go and see Mrs. Oakshott in the morning after all[9]," Holmes said. "Let's find out who this man is, Watson!"

We followed the man and came up[10] close behind him. Holmes touched the man's back which caused him to leap into the air[11]. His face had turned white from the surprise.

"Who are you? What do you want?" he cried.

"Excuse me. But I heard you asking about geese before? I think I might be able to help you."

27

He looked very suspiciously[1] at Holmes and me.

"Who are you and what do you have to do with the geese?" he asked.

"This is Watson and I am Sherlock Holmes. I know that you are looking for a goose that was sold to a Mr. Henry Baker. Mr. Baker bought the goose from the Alpha Inn which had bought the goose from Mr. Breckinridge. Mr. Breckinridge had initially[2] bought the goose from Mrs. Oakshott."

The man's appearance[3] changed. He looked very happy and cried, "Oh! You are the very people I need!"

"Come over to my house," said Holmes. "What is your name?"

---

1. **suspiciously** [sə`spɪʃəsli] (adv.) 猜疑地
2. **initially** [ɪ`nɪʃəli] (adv.) 最初
3. **appearance** [ə`pɪrəns] (n.) 外貌；外觀
4. **hesitate** [`hezɪteɪt] (v.) 猶豫
5. **for a bit** 有一點
6. **be employed** 受雇
7. **cab** [kæb] (n.) 計程車
8. **eventually** [ɪ`ventʃuəli] (adv.) 最後
9. **join** [dʒɔɪn] (v.) 參加；加入
10. **ride** [raɪd] (n.) 乘坐；搭乘

The man hesitated[4] for a bit[5] and then said, "John Robinson."

"I would like to know your real name," said Holmes, calmly.

The man looked very guilty and then said, "James Ryder."

"Yes, right! You are employed[6] at the Hotel Cosmopolitan. Why don't we take this cab? We will talk about everything when we get to my home," said Holmes.

The man seemed to be a little afraid. He hesitated to get into the cab[7] for a while but eventually[8], he decided to join[9] us. We were all quiet during the ride[10].

28

"Here we are!" said Holmes cheerily[1].

"You look cold, Mr. Ryder. Please take that seat[2] by the fire. . . Now! I guess you really want to know what happened to your goose?" Holmes asked him.

"Oh yes, sir!"

"Well, it came here. It was very strange. I've never seen a dead goose lay an egg[3] before especially when it is a bright blue egg like this one."

1. **cheerily** [ˋtʃɪrɪli] (adv.) 興高采烈地
2. **take a seat** 坐下
3. **lay an egg** 生蛋
4. **hold up** 舉起
5. **over** [ˋouvə(r)] (adv.) 結束地

6. **be onto you** 〔口〕追查你的違法活動
7. **upon/on** (prep.) 在……後 立即（後接動名詞）
8. **faint** [feɪnt] (v.) 暈倒
9. **a small amount of** 少量的

Holmes held up[4] the blue carbuncle.
"It's over[5], Ryder. We are onto you[6]."

Upon[7] hearing that, the man started to faint[8].

We gave the man a small amount of[9]
brandy[10] and he quickly came to[11].

"I know almost everything," said Holmes.
"It is a terrible thing that you have done to
Horner. You knew about his previous
conviction[12] and you knew that he would be
the first suspect[13]. You set up the whole thing
for Horner to go into the Countess's room and
then be blamed for[14] the theft."

The man was now quite terrified[15] and
begged, "Please don't tell the police. I'm really
not a bad man."

"Now that you've been caught you are sorry
but you didn't care whether Horner suffered[16]
in jail or not," Holmes said.

"Alright! I'll leave the country. Please don't
tell the police."

10. **brandy** ['brændi] (n.)
白蘭地酒
11. **come to** 甦醒過來
12. **previous conviction**
前科；以前的定罪
13. **suspect** ['sʌspekt] (n.)
嫌疑犯
14. **blame for**
對某壞事應負責任
15. **terrified** ['terɪfaɪd] (a.)
恐懼的
16. **suffer** ['sʌfə(r)] (v.) 受苦

29

"Tell us everything that happened," demanded[1] Holmes.

"Alright! Alright! I stole[2] the stone but even after the police arrested Horner, I knew I was not safe. I had to get the stone away[3] because the police might search[4] me at any time."

"I quickly went to my sister's place[5]. She is Mrs. Oakshott. As you already know, she raises geese. At my sister's place, I decided I would go to Kilburn. A man I know lives there and he is a criminal[6]. I knew he would be able to help me sell the stone. But I was worried that the police would find the stone on me."

"My sister had promised[7] to give me a goose so I chose one of her geese. The one I chose was a big one with a bar[8] on its tail. I opened up its beak[9] and forced[10] the stone down its throat. I had to struggle with[11] it, and it jumped out of my arms and went back to the other geese. I caught it again and took it to Kilburn."

1. **demand** [dɪˋmænd]
   (v.) 要求
2. **steal** [stiːl] (v.) 偷竊
3. **get . . . away** 拿走……
4. **search** [sɜːrtʃ] (v.) 搜查
5. **place** [pleɪs] (n.)
   住所；寓所
6. **criminal** [ˋkrɪmɪnl] (n.)
   罪犯

"My friend and I cut the goose open but then I was horrified[12]. There was no stone. I quickly went back to my sister's house. I asked her if there were any similar birds and she said that there was one. The problem was though that she had already sold it to Breckinridge. You know the rest of the story."

7. **promise** [ˋprɑːmɪs] (v.) 允諾；作出保證
8. **bar** [bɑː(r)] (n.) 條紋
9. **beak** [biːk] (n.) 鳥嘴
10. **force** [fɔːrs] (v.) 用力推進
11. **struggle with** 奮鬥
12. **horrified** [ˋhɔːrɪfaɪd] (a.) 恐懼的

81

🎧 30

    Holmes and I listened to his story. Holmes didn't say anything, but he had a solemn[1] look[2] on his face.

    Suddenly, he stood up, threw the door open and shouted, "Get out[3]!"

    The man was quite frightened but relieved[4].

    "Oh! Thank you sir! God bless you[5]!" he said.

1. **solemn** [`sɑːləm] (a.) 嚴肅的
2. **look** [luk] (n.) 眼色；表情
3. **get out**（用於命令句）走開；滾開
4. **relieved** [rɪ`liːvd] (a.) 放心的；寬慰的
5. **God bless you!** 上帝祝福你！
6. **trip** [trɪp] (v.) 〔書〕輕快地走（或跑）(trip-tripped-tripped)
7. **rush** [rʌʃ] (n.) 衝；奔；忽忙
8. **get away** 走開，離開

The man quickly ran out and down the stairs. We could hear him trip[6] down the stairs in his rush[7] to get away[8]. I looked at Holmes inquisitively[9].

"Watson, I am never paid for[10] my work by the police. The stone will be returned to the Countess. Ryder will not testify against[11] Horner now, so he will be released[12] from prison. Ryder will not do anything wrong again. So I see no point in[13] sending him to jail. It will just make life difficult for his own family.

It is the Christmas season. We have to find it in our hearts to forgive[14], especially at this time of year. Now I think it's time we looked into another bird. Let's hope our dinner won't start us on another goose chase."

9. **inquisitively** [ɪnˋkwɪzətɪvli] (adv.) 十分好奇地
10. **pay for** 受支付做某事 (pay-paid-paid)
11. **testify against** 作對……不利的證明
12. **release** [rɪˋliːs] (v.) 釋放
13. **point in**（作某事）有意義 （後接動名詞）
14. **forgive** [fərˋgɪv] (v.) 原諒；寬恕 (forgive-forgave-forgiven)

A Fill in the blanks with proper words

in	up	off	in on

1 call _____ •   • **a** To result in

2 pick _____ •   • **b** To leave by running on foot

3 knock _____ •   • **c** To give

4 run _____ •   • **d** To make something fall by hitting it

5 end _____ •   • **e** To visit someone

6 put _____ •   • **f** To take something from the ground

B Rewrite the sentences in subordinate clauses.

1 "I've never seen a dead goose lay an egg before," Holmes said.

→ Holmes said _____.

2 Holmes laughed and said, "That will be an easy five pounds for me."

→ Holmes laughed and said _____

_____.

3 "A man I know lives there and he is a criminal," Ryder said.

→ Ryder said _____.

C Rearrange the sentences in chronological order.

1. Mr. Henry Baker visited Holmes at his place.
2. Peterson rushed into the house, out of breath.
3. Peterson went to put an advertisement into the newspapers.
4. Holmes had been looking at a dirty, torn hat.
5. Mr. Baker said he got the goose from the Alpha Inn.
6. They read that John Horner was arrested by the police.
7. Holmes told Watson about the man who was attacked.

_____ ⇨ _____ ⇨ _____ ⇨ _____ ⇨ _____ ⇨ _____ ⇨ _____

D Fill in the blanks with the given words.

> pick up   owner   tag   run off   problem

"The gang of thieves ❶ _____ and left the hat and the goose. Peterson was left to ❷ _____ the hat and the goose." "Peterson went in search of the ❸ _____, didn't he?" I asked. "Well, that is the ❹ _____. We know who the owner is. There was a ❺ _____ tied to the goose with the owner's name, 'For Mrs. Henry Baker.'"

A Scandal[1] in Bohemia[2]

波希米亞醜聞案

Chapter One

The Photograph[3]

One unusual[4] characteristic[5] of Sherlock Holmes is that he has never cared for[6] women. There was, perhaps, one woman who left a great impression[7] on him. Her name was Irene Adler. Even though he did not love her, he never forgot her. However, I will not begin this story with her description[8]. I will discuss some other important details[9] first.

After not having seen Holmes for quite some time due to[10] my marriage, I decided to call on him. Holmes welcomed me very warmly[11].

"Watson! It's been such a long time! Come in! Come in! It's lucky that you dropped by[12] tonight. Take a look at this! It arrived just today, but there is no name, date or address."

It was a short letter. It read:

An individual[13] will visit you tonight at 7:45 p.m. The purpose[14] is to be kept a secret. As you have helped many other people, some being very important, I am hoping that you will be able to help me too.

1. **scandal** [ˋskændl]
   (n.) 醜聞
2. **Bohemia** [boˋhimɪə] (n.)
   波希米亞（捷克西部地區）
3. **photograph** [ˋfoutəgræf]
   (n.) 相片
4. **unusual** [ʌnˋjuːʒuəl] (a.)
   不尋常的
5. **characteristic**
   [kærəktəˋrɪstɪk] (n.)
   特質；特徵
6. **care for** 喜歡（某人）
7. **impression** [ɪmˋprɛʃən]
   (n.) 印象
8. **description** [dɪˋskrɪpʃən]
   (n.) 描述
9. **detail(s)** [ˋdiːteɪl(z)]
   (n.) 細節
10. **due to** 由於
11. **warmly** [ˋwɔːrmli] (adv.)
    熱烈地；熱情地
12. **drop by** 順便拜訪
13. **individual** [ɪndɪˋvɪdʒuəl]
    (n.) 個人
14. **purpose** [ˋpɜːrpəs] (n.)
    目的；意圖

32

"Well, Watson! What do you think of the paper?" he asked me.

I tried to think like Holmes. "The paper is of very high quality[1]. I am guessing that the person is rich. It's a strange paper."

"Yes. By examining it closely, it's not English. Perhaps a German wrote the letter. The paper was made in Bohemia. There's the sound of horses outside now. Maybe that's our mysterious visitor," said he.

1. **quality** [ˋkwɑːləti] (n.) 品質
2. **opinion** [əˋpɪnjən] (n.) 意見；見解
3. **whatever** [wɑːtˋevə(r)] (pron.) 不管什麼
4. **knock** [nɑːk] (n.) 敲；擊
5. **instruct** [ɪnˋstrʌkt] (v.) 告知
6. **finely** [ˋfaɪnli] (adv.) 極好地
7. **mask** [mæsk] (n.) 面具
8. **keep it a secret** 保守秘密

"Would you like me to leave, Holmes?"

"No, please stay. I would like your opinion[2] on whatever[3] the person wants," he told me.

Then, there was a knock[4] on the door.

"Come in!" Holmes instructed[5].

A mysterious looking man entered. He was finely[6] dressed and wore a mask[7] over his face.

"I am Count von Kramm from Bohemia. I have come on some very important business," the man said. "You must promise to keep it a secret[8]."

"Of course we will keep your secret," Holmes and I promised.

One Point Lesson

◆ The paper is **of** high **quality**. 這是高質感的紙。

of+ 形容詞 + **quality**：有……的品質
of + 形容詞 + 名詞：有……的性質

e.g. They are **of** the same **age**. 他們同齡。

33

"I have come with a message from a royal[1] family. Their identity[2] must be kept a secret, so I am wearing a mask. If you cannot help, one of the most important families in Europe will be in great trouble[3]. It will cause a very big scandal. This is the House of[4] Ormstein, King of Bohemia."

Holmes listened and replied, "I understand, Your Majesty[5]."

This shocked[6] the man who suddenly jumped up and pulled[7] the mask from his face.

"But how could you know that I am the King?" He threw the mask on the ground. "Why do I have to hide it? I am the king. I am Wilhelm von Ormstein, King of Bohemia. I couldn't trust another person with[8] my story so I came to ask you for your help myself."

1. **royal** [ˋrɔɪəl] (a.) 王室的
2. **identity** [aɪˋdɛntəti] (n.) 身分
3. **in trouble** 處困難中
4. **the house of** 某家族（尤指皇族或貴族）
5. **Your Majesty** 陛下
6. **shock** [ʃɑːk] (v.) 使震驚
7. **pull** [pʊl] (v.) 拉開
8. **trust with** 把某物託付給某人
9. **back** [bæk] (adv.) 以前

"Please continue," Holmes said.

"There is a woman named Irene Adler who I met five years ago. We. . ."

"Irene Adler!" Holmes interrupted. "A singer born in 1850, a very beautiful woman living in London. You loved her, didn't you? You wrote her love letters but then you left her. And now you need those letters."

"Yes, that's right. But she also has a photograph with both of us in it. It was a mistake to give it to her. I was a stupid foolish young man back[9] then," the King said.

93

34

"Have you tried to get the photograph back[1]?" Holmes asked.

"Yes, several times."

Holmes began to laugh, "What is she going to do with the picture?"

"I am engaged[2] to be married to Clotilde Lothman von Saxe-Meningen, the daughter of the King of Scandinavia. If she finds out[3] I am connected[4] to Irene Adler, she will never marry me. We must marry. We are the two most important families in Europe. But Irene . . . she is beautiful, but she was very angry when I left her. She doesn't want me to marry another woman, and I know she will send the family the photograph to stop my marriage."

1. **get A back** 取回 A
2. **engaged** 和……訂婚
3. **find out** 發現
4. **connect (to)** 有關係
5. **inform A of** 通知 A 某事
6. **assure** [əˋʃʊr] (v.) 向……保證
7. **lodge** [lɑːdʒ] (n.) 旅舍
8. **avenue** [ˋævənuː] (n.) 大街；大道

"Don't worry! We will find the photograph. I will inform you of[5] what happens," assured[6] Holmes.

The King put a bag on the table. "Here is one thousand pounds. I must have that photograph. Here is her address: Biony Lodge[7], Serpentine Avenue[8], St. John's Wood, London."

"Good evening, Your Majesty."

The King left and Holmes said to me, "Come back at 3 p.m. tomorrow."

Is Arthur Conan Doyle a Murderer?

The strangest story about Sir Arthur Conan Doyle is that he murdered a colleague[1] to steal the idea for his most famous Sherlock Holmes novel. In 2000, a researcher[2] named Rodger-Garrick Steele made this claim[3] against Doyle. Steele spent eleven years researching[4] the relationship between Doyle and another writer named Fletcher Robinson.

According to Steele, Doyle loved Robinson's wife very much, and the idea for one of Doyle's most famous novels, "The Hound of the Baskervilles," was actually Robinson's idea. Robinson had tried unsuccessfully to publish[5] the same story in a novel called "An Adventure on Dartmoor."

Doyle, who was trained in medicine[6], had him take laudanum[7], a poison that causes symptoms[8] very similar to those caused by typhoid[9]. Robinson died in 1907 at the age of 36, supposedly[10] of typhoid.

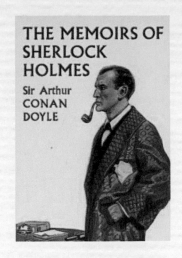

Of course, this theory caused an uproar[11] around the world. Fans of Sherlock Holmes were extremely upset. To finally put a rest[12] to this controversy[13], Steele tried to get Robinson's remains[14] examined[15]. Modern medical tests can prove whether he was poisoned[16] or not. As of today, no decision has been made to do this, and so the whole controversy remains a mystery — ironically one very similar to a Sherlock Holmes story!

---

1. **colleague** [ˋkɑːliːg] (n.) 同事
2. **researcher** [rɪˋsɜːrtʃər] (n.) 研究者
3. **claim** [kleɪm] (v.) 宣稱
4. **research** [ˋriːsɜːrtʃ] (v.) 研究
5. **publish** [ˋpʌblɪʃ] (v.) 出版
6. **medicine** [ˋmedɪsn] (n.) 醫學
7. **laudanum** [ˋlɔːdənəm] (n.) 〔藥〕鴉片酊
8. **symptom** [ˋsɪmptəm] (n.) 症狀
9. **typhoid** [ˋtaɪfɔɪd] (n.) 〔醫〕傷寒症
10. **supposedly** [səˋpouzɪdli] (adv.) 根據推測；據稱
11. **uproar** [ˋʌprɔː(r)] (n.) 騷亂；騷動
12. **put a rest** 停止
13. **controversy** [ˋkɑːntrəvɜːrsi] (n.) 爭議
14. **remains** [rɪˋmeɪnz] (n.) 遺體
15. **examine** [ɪgˋzæmɪn] (v.) 檢查
16. **poison** [ˋpɔɪzn] (v.) 毒死

Chapter Two

Holmes Gets Outsmarted[1]

I arrived at Holmes's place. He was not there at three but at four a very strange servant[2] entered the room. He looked old and dirty but then I realized it was Holmes.

"What are you doing?" I asked.

He was smiling and said, "Oh, Watson. Today has been very interesting. Servants are always willing to[3] talk. I have discovered[4] so much outside Irene's house. The most interesting thing is her lawyer[5] friend, Godfrey Norton. He happened to[6] arrive while I was there. I watched them but then he quickly left and took a taxi[7]. She came out very soon after and followed[8] in another taxi.

I had to follow them so I took a third taxi. They went to the Church of St. Monica. I entered the church and Norton called out[9] to me, 'Come here quickly.'"

"What did you do?" I asked.

"I helped marry them," he replied.

1. **outsmart** [aut`smɑːrt] (v.)
   比……更聰明；用計謀打敗
2. **servant** [`sɜːrvənt] (n.) 僕人
3. **be willing to** 樂意；願意
4. **discover** [dɪ`skʌvə(r)]
   (v.) 發現
5. **lawyer** [`lɔːjə(r)] (n.) 律師
6. **happen to** 碰巧
7. **take a taxi** 搭計程車
8. **follow** [`fɑːlou] (v.) 跟隨
9. **call out** 大聲地喊

36

"She married him! What is the next plan of action[1]?" I asked again.

"Well, tonight Watson, will you help me without[2] asking any questions?"

"Holmes, of course I will help you!"

"We will go to her home at Biony Lodge at 7 p.m. She will invite[3] me into her home. I want you to wait outside the sitting room by the window. Keep this smoke stick[4] with you while you wait. When you see my hand, throw it through the window. After you throw it into the room, shout, 'Fire!' There will be no fire. The room will simply[5] fill up with[6] smoke. After you do that, wait for me on the street corner."

"Alright! I can do all of that," I said.

Holmes and I prepared for that night. Holmes changed his whole appearance[7] to look like a completely[8] different man. We went to the house and noticed a lot of people chatting[9] and smoking outside.

"I am sure that the photograph is in her house. I don't think she would keep it in a place like a bank. I think that the King's men just didn't know where to look," Holmes said to me.

"So then how will you find it?" I asked.

"I will wait for her to show me."

1. **action** [`ækʃn] (n.) 行動
2. **without** [wɪ`ðaʊt] (prep.)
   沒有（做某事）
   （後接動名詞）
3. **invite** [ɪn`vaɪt] (v.) 邀請
4. **smoke stick** 冒煙的棍子
5. **simply** [`sɪmpli] (adv)
   僅僅；只不過
6. **fill up with** 以某物裝滿
7. **appearance** [ə`pɪrəns] (n.)
   外表；外貌
8. **completely** [kəm`pliːtli]
   (adv.) 完全地
9. **chat** [tʃæt] (v.) 聊天

37

As we were talking, a taxi arrived. Irene Norton stepped out[1]. Just at that moment, a fight broke out[2] among the men standing in front of her house. Irene was in the middle of[3] it, getting pushed around[4]. Holmes ran off to give her some assistance[5]. He was helping her when he got hit. He fell to the ground[6] and there was blood on his face.

By this time, Irene had hurried away[7]. She turned around and saw Holmes on the ground.

"Is he injured[8]?" she asked.

"I think he's dead," said one person.

"He's not dead, just hurt," said another person.

"Bring him into my home," Irene said.

I saw all of this happen and went to wait outside the sitting room window. I watched what happened inside. Holmes held up his hand and then I threw the smoke stick inside. I shouted "Fire," and the room very quickly filled with smoke.

1. **step out**
   走出（此指走出計程車）
   (step-stepped-stepped)
2. **break out** 爆發；突然發生
   (break-broke-broken)
3. **in the middle of**
   在……當中
4. **get pushed around**
   受推擠
5. **assistance** [əˋsɪstəns] (n.)
   援助；幫助
6. **fall to the ground** 倒地
7. **hurry away** 趕緊離開
8. **injured** [ˋɪndʒɚd]
   (a.) 受傷的

I went to wait for Holmes on the street corner and Holmes appeared about 10 minutes later.

"Did you get the photograph?" I asked.

"No, but she showed me," he told me.

"How did you manage[1] that?" I asked.

Holmes just laughed and said, "I paid those people to start a fight in the street. That got me into Irene's home. Then, you threw the smoke stick into the room. When there is a fire, people always run to get their most valuable[2] possessions[3]. I watched as she ran to get her photograph. It's in her cupboard[4]. We will go with the King to get it tomorrow."

Holmes talked as we walked back to his home on Baker Street. We were walking to the front[5] entrance[6] of his house when a young man rushed[7] past[8] us and said, "Good evening, Mr. Sherlock Holmes."

The voice[9] was very familiar[10] to Holmes. "Whose is that voice? I can't put a face to it," Holmes said to me.

We said good night to one another and agreed to meet the next day.

1. **manage** [`mænɪdʒ] (v.) 設法做到
2. **valuable** [`væljuəbl] (a.) 有價值的
3. **possessions** [pə`zeʃnz] (n.) 所有物；財產
4. **cupboard** [`kʌbərd] (n.) 廚櫃；壁櫥
5. **front** [frʌnt] (a.) 前面的；正面的
6. **entrance** [`entrəns] (n.) 入口；門口
7. **rush** [rʌʃ] (v.) 衝；奔
8. **past** [pæst] (prep.) 經過
9. **voice** [vɔɪs] (n.) 聲音
10. **familiar** [fə`mɪliə(r)] (a.) 熟悉的

🎧 39

In the morning, we went to Biony Lodge with the King. A servant greeted[1] us at the door and asked, "Are you Mr. Sherlock Holmes?"

Holmes was very surprised but said, "Yes."

"Mrs. Norton asked me to tell you that she and her husband left England this morning. They never plan to return."

This new information left us all in[2] great shock[3].

"The photograph! Whatever will I do!" exclaimed the King. We all rushed past the servant into the sitting room. Holmes opened the cupboard. There was a photograph but it was only of her alone.

There was also a letter for Holmes. It read:

1. **greet** [griːt] (v.)
   問候；迎接；招呼
2. **leave A in**
   置 A 於（某狀態）
3. **in shock** 處震驚中
4. **suspicious** [sə`spɪʃəs] (a.)
   疑心的；多疑的

Dear Mr. Sherlock Holmes,

You had a very good plan to get the photograph. After the fire, I started to become suspicious [4]. I had heard that the King had employed you to get the photograph back. Then I thought that it may have been you who started the fight and the fire. I dressed as a man and followed you back to your home on Baker Street just to be certain [5].

My husband and I quickly decided to leave England. I know that the King is worried about the photograph but please tell him that I will not use it against [6] him. I have married a better man than the King and he is now free to marry the daughter of the King of Scandinavia. I am leaving this other photograph of me instead [7] which he may take.

Mrs. Irene Norton

5. **certain** [ˈsɜːrtn] (a.)
   確鑿的；無疑的

6. **against** [əˈɡenst] (prep.)
   反對

7. **instead** [ɪnˈsted] (adv.)
   作為替代

"She is a very clever woman," cried Holmes.

"Yes, I should have married her after all[1]," declared[2] the King.

Holmes looked very serious.

"Your Majesty! Unfortunately[3] I have failed in[4] my attempt[5] to retrieve[6] your photograph. I am very sorry."

"Irene has promised in this letter never to use the photograph against me. I trust[7] her promise. I am free to marry the Princess of Scandinavia now. I am very grateful[8] for what you have done," the King told Holmes.

"There is one thing I would like," said Holmes.

"Yes, Mr. Holmes, what can I do for you?"

"I would like the photograph of the only woman who has outsmarted me," he told the King.

"Yes, you may have it!"

So Holmes took the photograph and the King married Clotilde Lothman von Saxe-Meningen.

1. **after all** 畢竟
2. **declare** [dɪˋkler] (v.)
   宣告；表示
3. **unfortunately**
   [ʌnˋfɔːrtʃənətli] (adv.)
   不幸地
4. **fail in** 失敗
5. **attempt** [əˋtempt] (n.)
   試圖；企圖
6. **retrieve** [rɪˋtriːv] (v.)
   收回；重新得到
7. **trust** [trʌst] (v.) 信任
8. **grateful** [ˋgreɪtfəl] (a.)
   感謝的；感激的

A True or False.

T F **1** The King of Bohemia wanted to marry Irene Adler.

T F **2** Watson hadn't seen Holmes because he was married now.

T F **3** Irene Adler didn't want the King to marry another woman.

T F **4** Holmes had never heard of Irene before.

T F **5** The King didn't trust anyone else except Holmes.

T F **6** Holmes usually worked on cases for free.

B Rearrange the sentences in chronological order.

1 A mysterious man wearing a mask entered the house.

2 The man said he had tried to get the photograph back.

3 Watson called in on Holmes after a long time.

4 The man left one thousand pounds on the table.

5 The man said that he had sent love letters to Irene.

6 Holmes was reading a mysterious letter.

_____ ⇨ _____ ⇨ _____ ⇨ _____ ⇨ _____ ⇨ _____

C Choose the correct answer.

1 Why was Holmes dressed as a servant?

    (a) Because it was his new job.

    (b) Because it was his disguise.

    (c) Because he usually dressed as a servant.

2 What did the woman promise not to do in her letter?

    (a) Marry another man.

    (b) Send the photograph to the Saxe-Meningen family.

    (c) Leave the country.

D Fill in the blanks with the given words.

description	warmly	characteristic
discuss	marriage	impression

One unusual **1** _____ of Sherlock Holmes is that he has never cared for women. There was, perhaps, one woman who left a great **2** _____ on him. Her name was Irene Adler. Even though he did not love her, he never forgot her. However, I will not begin this story with her **3** _____.

I will **4** _____ some other important details first. After not having seen Holmes for quite some time due to my **5** _____, I decided to call in on him. Holmes welcomed me very **6** _____.

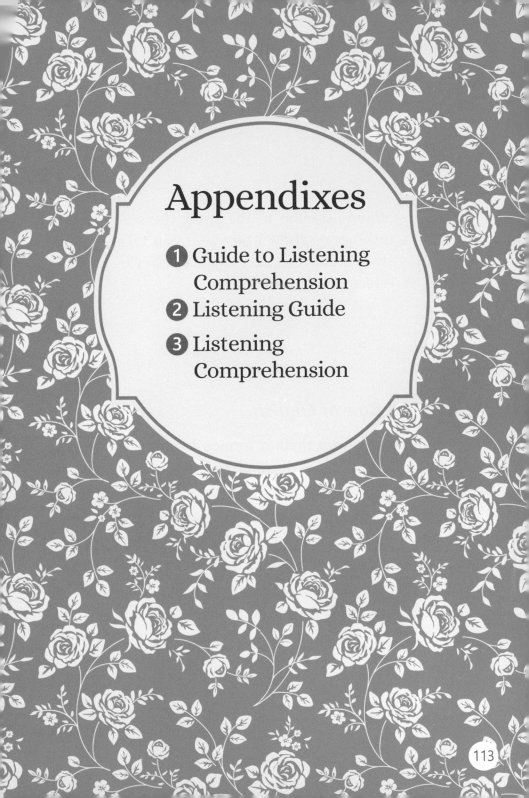

Appendixes

1 Guide to Listening Comprehension
2 Listening Guide
3 Listening Comprehension

Guide to Listening Comprehension

 When listening to the story, use some of the techniques shown below. If you take time to study some phonetic characteristics of English, listening will be easier.

Get in the flow of English.

English creates a rhythm formed by combinations of strong and weak stress intonations. Each word has its particular stress that combines with other words to form the overall pattern of stress or rhythm in a particular sentence.

When you are speaking and listening to English, it is essential to get in the flow of the rhythm of English. It takes a lot of practice to get used to such a rhythm. So, you need to start by identifying the stressed syllable in a word.

Listen for the strongly stressed words and phrases.

In English, key words and phrases that are essential to the meaning of a sentence are stressed louder. Therefore, pay attention to the words stressed with a higher pitch. When listening to an English recording for the first time, what matters most is to listen for a general understanding of what you hear. Do not try to hear every single word. Most of the unstressed words are articles or auxiliary verbs, which don't play an important role in the general context. At this level, you can ignore them.

Pay attention to liaisons.

In reading English, words are written with a space between them. There isn't such an obvious guide when it comes to listening to English. In oral English, there are many cases when the sounds of words are linked with adjacent words.

For instance, let's think about the phrase "**take off**," which can be used in "take off your clothes." "Take off your clothes" doesn't sound like [teɪk ɔːf] with each of the words completely and clearly separated from the others. Instead, it sounds as if almost all the words in context are slurred together, [ˈteɪkɔːf], for a more natural sound.

Shadow the voice of the native speaker.

Finally, you need to mimic the voice of the native speaker. Once you are sure you know how to pronounce all the words in a sentence, try to repeat them like an echo. Listen to the book again, but this time you should try a fun exercise while listening to the English.

This exercise is called "shadowing." The word "shadow" means a dark shade that is formed on a surface. When used as a verb, the word refers to the action of following someone or something like a shadow. In this exercise, pretend you are a parrot and try to shadow the voice of the native speaker.

Try to mimic the reader's voice by speaking at the same speed, with the same strong and weak stresses on words, and pausing or stopping at the same points.

Experts have already proven this technique to be effective. If you practice this shadowing exercise, your English speaking and listening skills will improve by leaps and bounds. While shadowing the native speaker, don't forget to pay attention to the meaning of each phrase and sentence.

Listen to what you want to shadow many times. Start out by just trying to shadow a few words or a sentence.

 Mimic the CD out loud. You can shadow everything the speaker says as if you are singing a round, or you also can speak simultaneously with the recorded voice of the native speaker.

 As you practice more, try to shadow more. For instance, shadow a whole sentence or paragraph instead of just a few words.

2 Listening Guide

以下為《福爾摩斯》各章節的前半部。一開始若能聽清楚發音，之後就沒有聽力的負擔。先聽過摘錄的章節，之後再反覆聆聽括弧內單字的發音，並仔細閱讀各種發音的說明。以下都是以英語的典型發音為基礎，所做的簡易說明，即使這裡未提到的發音，也可以配合音檔反覆聆聽，如此一來聽力必能更上層樓。

Chapter One page 16–17 🎧 41

I awoke very early one morning in April 1883. Sherlock Holmes and I were living together. I (**1**) (　　　) the clock and saw that it was only seven. Usually Holmes liked to sleep in late, but he was already dressed, hovering over me. I looked up at him in surprise.

"(**2**) (　　　) (　　　), Holmes?" I asked. "Is there a fire?"

"No, there is a woman here. I think it is a case. I know you will (**3**) (　　　) hear everything from the beginning, Watson," he said.

I quickly got dressed and (**4**) (　　　) with Holmes. We saw a lady in the sitting room. She (**5**) stood up when we entered the room. She was dressed in black and her expression was very grave.

❶ **looked at:** looked 的 -ed 接在 k 後面，發無聲的音，正確發音為 [lukt]。

❷ **What is it:** is 與前面的 what 形成連音，使 t 位於兩個母音之間而發出介於 [t] 和 [d] 的有聲子音，a lot of 即為另一例。三字連音聽起來有如快速念完一個字，是美語常見的特色。

❸ **want to:** want 的 t 和 to 的 t 連再一起發音，此時 to 的音聽起來就像 [t]，在英語中若相鄰的兩個子音連在一起時，只需發音一次。

❹ **went downstairs:** went 的 -nt 與 downstairs 的 d 連在一起發音，[t] 因屬無聲子音，又位於兩個有聲子音 [d] 和 [n] 之間，故常省略掉，連音時聽起來就像是 wendownstairs。

❺ **immediately:** immediately 中 -tely 的無聲子音 [t]，因在有聲子音 [l] 之前又位於輕音節 -diate- 的末尾，所以發音極輕微。

"Good morning! I am Sherlock Holmes and this is Dr. Watson. He is my dear friend and (**❶**)," Holmes said. "We (**❷**) (   ) (   ) hear everything."

We all sat down.

"I am Helen Stoner. I am living with my (**❸**), Dr. Grimesby Roylott," she explained. "The Roylott's have lived at Stoke Moran for centuries, but now my stepfather is the last living Roylott. The family was once very wealthy."

Holmes nodded. "I know the name," said he.

Miss Stoner (**❹**) (   ). "However, because of a long line of terrible men, the family fortune is all gone. There is only the little land and the two-hundred-year-old house left. My stepfather knew that there was no money for him to live on. So he (**❺**) (   ) (   ) a doctor and then went to India. When my mother met Dr. Roylott there, my father had only been dead for one year. Julia, my twin-sister, and I were only two years old (**❻**) (   ) (   )."

1 **associate:** associate 此處為名詞，所以 -ciate 發音為 [-ʃiət]，動詞則為 [-ʃieɪt]。另 a 若是第一個字母又位於輕音節，常弱化為 [ə]。

2 **would like to:** would 的 d 與 like 的 l 接在一起，雖然同為有聲子音，但因屬音節末尾，所以口語上的發音就變得輕微，甚至省略，形成兩個 [l] 連音只發一個 [l] 的現象，聽起來就像是 woulike。

To 因屬意義較不重要的功能詞（像是介係詞、助動詞、代名詞），所以發音變得很輕，母音由 [tu] 中的 [u] 弱化成 [ə]，發 [tə]。

3 **stepfather:** 重音在第一音節。Step 的 p 與 father 的 f 雖同屬無聲子音，但因 -fa- 是次重音節，而 p 又是位於音節末尾，如同其他位於音節末尾的子音一樣，在口語上發音就變得極輕，甚至省略，聽起來好像 e 與 f 之間有停頓一樣。

4 **went on:** on 與前面 went 的 t 連音，因 t 前有有聲子音，後有母音，所以如同位於兩個母音之間一樣，t 發出介於 [t] 和 [d] 之間的閃音。此種類型發音在美語相當常見。

5 **studied to become:** to 因屬意義較不重要的功能詞（像是介係詞、助動詞、代名詞），所以發輕音，母音由 [tu] 中的 [u] 弱化成 [ə]，發 [tə]。

6 **at that time:** at 的 t 與 that 的第二個 t 雖同處音節末尾，省略情形卻稍有不同。at 的 t 後面接著重音節 that 的 th [ð]（有聲子音），又位於音節末尾，所以口語上發音極輕甚至省略。that 的第二個 t 接著後面 time 的 t，兩個 t 接鄰只發一個 [t] 音，如同 went to。三個字口語上連音聽起來就像 athatime。

Listening Comprehension

🎧 43 **A** Listen to the CD and choose the correct definition of character.

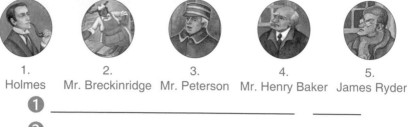

1.	2.	3.	4.	5.
Holmes	Mr. Breckinridge	Mr. Peterson	Mr. Henry Baker	James Ryder

1 _____ _____

2 _____ _____

3 _____ _____

4 _____ _____

5 _____ _____

🎧 44 **B** Listen to the CD and fill in the blanks with correct words.

1. Godfrey Norton and Irene Adler _____ _____ the church in different taxis.

2. Watson _____ _____ _____ throw a smoke stick into Irene Adler's sitting room.

3. The fight _____ _____ _____ Irene's house was planned.

4. People always worry about their most valuable possessions when _____ _____ _____ _____.

5. Holmes _____ _____ _____ _____ outsmart Irene Adler.

45

C Listen to the CD and choose the correct answer.

❶ _____?

    (a) He stole it from the Countess.

    (b) He fought with a man to get it.

    (c) He picked it up off the street.

❷ _____?

    (a) Because they didn't buy any geese.

    (b) Because many people had asked him about the geese.

    (c) Because they were annoying him.

❸ _____?

    (a) Someone stole it from him.

    (b) It got mixed up with some other geese.

    (c) It flew away.

46

D True or False.

T F ① ....

T F ② ....

T F ③ ....

T F ④ ....

T F ⑤ ....

Translation

亞瑟‧柯南‧道爾爵士（Sir Arthur Conan Doyle, 1859–1930），1859 年 5 月 22 日生於蘇格蘭愛丁堡，自幼接受嚴格的斯巴達式教育。母親瑪麗‧道爾（Mary Doyle）熱愛書本、擅長說故事，受其影響，亞瑟也喜愛閱讀與作文。

就讀愛丁堡大學醫學院時，他遇見許多將來成為作家的同校生，像是詹姆斯‧馬修‧巴利（James Barrie）和羅伯特‧路易斯‧史蒂文森（Robert Louis Stevenson）。然而，他最欽佩且影響他最深的是老師約瑟夫‧貝爾博士（Dr. Joseph Bell）。這位良醫擅長觀察、邏輯好、善推論且精於診斷，這些特質之後都呈現在名偵探福爾摩斯的身上。

在本科深耕幾年後，亞瑟決定試著書寫短篇小說。由於特別尊敬愛倫‧坡（Edgar Allen Poe）和埃米爾‧加博里歐（Émile Gaboriau），他撰寫懸疑小說，專心致意塑造著自己筆下的鮮明角色。最終他創作出史上最著名的偵探：夏洛克‧福爾摩斯。

1887 年，以《血字的研究》（A Study in Scarlet）開始，亞瑟出版了懸疑小說系列，福爾摩斯和華生醫生在其中扮演重要的角色。其後，他在月刊上發表的短篇小說受到讀者熱烈歡迎，也替之後成為人氣作家墊基。

1892 年，他將故事收集成《福爾摩斯冒險史》（The Adventures of Sherlock Holmes）。1894 年，他原想以《福爾摩斯回憶錄》（The Memories of Sherlock Holmes）作為系列終結，然而在讀者要求下，1902 年又出版了《巴斯克維爾的獵犬》（The Hound of the Baskervilles）。之後他撰寫《福爾摩斯歸來記》（The Return of Sherlock Holmes）與其他故事延續系列。

1902 年他以軍醫身分參與波耳戰爭，因表現傑出而封爵。亞瑟‧柯南‧道爾於 1930 年 7 月 7 日在家人圍繞下去世，他向妻子交代遺言後，便「啟程往最偉大壯麗的冒險」。

〈斑繩記〉

某天，和父親同住的一對雙胞胎姊妹遭遇懸案，姐姐被殺身亡。妹妹海倫擔心生命受威脅，前來求助福爾摩斯。福爾摩斯憑直覺感應到犯人的真實身分，潛入海倫的住處，而在房裡出現的是……

〈藍寶石案〉

案情從福爾摩斯公寓的門房，在聖誕派對的歸途上，意外撿到一隻鵝和一頂帽子開始。那隻鵝的肚子裡有一顆美麗的藍寶石，許多人好奇寶石是如何放入鵝肚中。

〈波希米亞醜聞案〉

波希米亞國王親自拜訪福爾摩斯，要求替他拿回年輕時與愛人的合照。為了破案，福爾摩斯找上國王的舊情人，一陣混亂中，他竟成為她婚禮的伴郎。福爾摩斯能成功拿回照片嗎？

p. 12–13

夏洛克・福爾摩斯

夏洛克・福爾摩斯是世上最偉大、最有名的偵探之一。他只需看一下人們的少量衣物即可推度許多事情。他的觀察力和推論功夫不可思議，能力之強，解決了許多看似難解的謎。他貢獻辦案能力幫助身處困境的好人。這使他漸趨聞名。

華生醫生

　　華生醫生是福爾摩斯的老朋友。他不若福爾摩斯聰穎，常想不到福爾摩斯在忙什麼。但福爾摩斯喜歡讓華生醫生跟在身邊，也許是讓他當「推理顧問」吧。華生是位忠實的朋友，是福爾摩斯的好幫手。

海倫・史東納

　　我請求夏洛克・福爾摩斯協助，因為我怕性命不保。我姊姊死得不明不白，現在我怕我會是下一個受害者。

詹姆斯・萊德

　　我真的不是壞人。只因那石頭是這麼大又漂亮，我忍不住拿了它，卻把它弄丟了！我想我還不夠格犯罪。

波希米亞國王

　　你知道，身為國王總不會處處順遂。有時你得娶你不愛的人，我現在就是擔心前女友艾琳・艾德勒會試著阻止我娶那位皇室貴婦，希望夏洛克・福爾摩斯能幫我。

斑繩記

p. 16–17

［第一章］海倫・史東納

　　一八八三年四月一天一大早，我自夢中醒來。我和夏洛克・福爾摩斯同住。我看了時鐘，才七點。福爾摩斯常愛睡懶覺，但此時他已著完裝，在我身邊徘徊著。我驚訝地望著他。

我問：「福爾摩斯，什麼事啊？有火災嗎？」

他回答：「不，是來了位女士，應該有案子了。華生，我知道你會想聽整件事的始末的。」

我很快穿好衣服跟福爾摩斯下樓。我們在客廳看到一位小姐。我們進房間時她立刻起身。她一身黑衣，面色凝重。

福爾摩斯說：「您早！我是福爾摩斯，這位是華生醫生。他是我的好友與夥伴。我們想聽每件事。」

我們都坐了下來。

`p. 18–19` 她說明來意：「我叫海倫·史東納。我與我繼父格林斯比·羅伊洛特醫生同住。羅伊洛特家族已在斯多克莫蘭居住數百年，但如今只剩我繼父一脈。這家族曾經非常興旺。」

福爾摩斯點點頭說：「我知道這名字。」

史東納小姐繼續說：「不過因眾多的小人把持，家族的財富已空，只剩一小塊地和那棟兩百年屋齡的房子。

我繼父知道無錢財可供其維生了，所以他努力讀書成為一名醫生，去了印度。我母親在那裡遇見羅伊洛特醫生時，我父親才過世一年而已。我與雙胞胎姊姊茱莉亞那時只有兩歲。」

福爾摩斯問：「也許你母親有些錢？」

「噢，是的。她每年都存約一千英鎊。他們結婚時，我母親變更她的遺囑，把她所有的錢都留給他，但她確實在遺囑中說他得照顧茱莉亞和我。」

`p. 20–21` 「我們最後回來英國，母親不久隨即過世。我們全都搬到斯多克莫蘭居住。我們錢夠，但羅伊洛特在我們母親死後就變了，母親是在八年前的一場鐵路意外中身亡的。

他性情暴戾，和鄰居常有爭吵。他很壯，個性又古怪，大家都怕他。他只跟住在他土地上的一些吉普塞人說話。

他也養些野生動物，他從印度帶回一隻印度豹和一隻狒狒，任其四處遊蕩。

　　聽了我說這些，你可以想像我和我姊的日子並不好過。因為大家都怕我繼父，沒人願意幫我們工作，我們什麼事都得自己來。

　　茱莉亞已不幸過世，她死時只有三十歲，頭髮卻已經斑白，而我的頭髮也漸漸變白了。」

p. 22-23 「那麼你姊姊已經過世了？」

　　「她兩年前過世的，這就是我來找你的原因。我們極少離開斯多克莫蘭，但有時會去拜　　訪我們阿姨。有一次去拜訪時，茱莉亞遇到一位男士而陷入熱戀，而且已經談及婚事了。我們繼父從未開口反對這件婚事，但約十天後，茱莉亞死了。」

　　當她說著她的故事時，福爾摩斯一直靠著椅背，閉著眼睛靜靜聽著。這時，他迅速坐起身，說道：「告訴我們事情的每項細節。」

　　「每樣事我都可以一五一十告訴你們，事情彷彿是昨夜才發生過的，歷歷在目。就如我說過的，我們房子很舊了，而我們只住其中一邊的廂房。羅伊洛特醫生住第一間臥室，茱莉亞住第二間，我住第三間。各房之間無門相通，房門都是開向同一個長廊的。那夜，羅伊洛特醫生早早就回房了。我們知道他尚未入睡，因為茱莉亞聞到了他的雪茄菸味。他習慣在房中抽雪茄。」

p. 24-25 「茱莉亞一向討厭菸味，所以她就來我房裡。我們聊了好一會兒，主要是談她的婚禮。晚上十一點，她起身回房睡。就在她要離開時，她問：『你在凌晨有沒有聽到什麼口哨聲？』」

我告訴她我沒聽到任何聲音。然後她問我是否會在睡夢中吹口哨，我告訴她：『不會吧，你為什麼這麼問呢？』

　　她回答說，她凌晨三點夜深人靜時都會聽到一聲口哨聲。她睡眠很淺，一有聲音就會被吵醒。

　　她說她曾試著找出那聲音的來源。她不知道聲音是從隔壁房間還是外頭傳來的。我告訴她可能是吉普賽人的聲音，她說或許是吧，就回她房裡了。我聽到她走進房間，鎖上房門。」

p. 26–27 福爾摩斯問：「你晚上都會鎖上房門嗎？」

　　她回答：「會，晚上都會鎖門，我們很怕那隻印度豹和狒狒。」

　　「沒錯，這是想當然耳的。請繼續說下去。」

　　「那晚，我在床上翻來覆去，整夜都醒著。我們是雙胞胎，人家說雙胞胎心靈相通。我有一種不祥的恐懼感。那夜風很大，雨劈里啪啦擊著窗。接著我聽到一聲令人毛骨悚然的尖叫，我知道那是我姊的聲音。

　　我從床上跳起，就在往姊姊的房間跑時，聽到了一聲口哨聲，接著又聽到像一大堆金屬掉落的噹啷聲。姊姊慢慢地打開房門。

　　她的臉在走廊燈光下恐懼得慘白。我伸手攙住她，但就在那時她倒地不起。

　　她最後只說：『是繩子！有斑紋的繩子！』

　　她說完就死了。」

p. 28–29 福爾摩斯問：「你確定你聽到了口哨聲和噹啷聲？」

　　「噢，是的！我記得很清楚。」

　　「你姊姊當時穿著睡衣嗎？」

　　「是的，而且我們在她手中發現一個火柴盒。」

「這個案子警方怎麼說呢？」

史東納小姐回答：「他們徹底調查過，但就是沒找出她的死因。窗戶上橫栓鎖著，牆壁和地板都很厚，房門也是鎖上的，沒人能進去。」

福爾摩斯專注聽著，表情非常嚴肅。

他告訴她：「這種說法無法令人滿意。史東納小姐，請把整件事情說完吧。」

「嗯，我姊死後至今已兩年，我感到更加寂寞了，非常想念她。不過我最近遇到一位男士，他向我求婚。他叫波希·阿米塔吉，我們想在春天結婚。我繼父對我的婚事也沒有表示什麼意見。」

p. 30–31 「兩天前，繼父要我搬進茱莉亞的房間，因為他要整修我的房間。昨夜，我在茱莉亞的房間時，聽到了一聲低沉的口哨聲，那就是茱莉亞提過的那個聲音，而她就是在那晚死去的！我很害怕，立刻點上蠟燭，但我沒有看到任何異狀。

不用說，我昨晚失眠了。等天一亮，我很快穿好衣服就來這兒了。」

福爾摩斯坐在椅子上思索著。過了一會兒，他說：「這事非同小可，我們下午就去斯多克莫蘭。我們怎麼進去房子而又不會讓醫生知道呢？」

她告訴他們：「他今天一整天都不在家。」

「那好，我們下午就過去。我建議你現在回去等我們。」

史東納小姐隨即離開。

p. 32–33 ## 夏洛克‧福爾摩斯，真有其人？

亞瑟‧柯南‧道爾爵士在他的故事中提到福爾摩斯的許多事蹟，好像真有其人一樣，有些人也相信確有此人！

如果你遇到福爾摩斯，會看到一位又瘦又高，約高一百八十五公分的男士。福爾摩斯有一個狹窄的鷹鉤鼻。每當他在揣度事情時，眉頭常常深鎖。

福爾摩斯住在他祖國英國倫敦市貝克街 221b 號的一棟公寓。他在一間醫學大學讀了兩年。

他在聖巴特醫院時，經由介紹和約翰‧華生醫生認識。華生隨後成為福爾摩斯最好的朋友與傳記作者。直到華生結婚前，他們都住在一起。福爾摩斯從未結婚，而事實上，他似乎不喜歡女人。

福爾摩斯信賴的房東哈德森太太，時常叨唸福爾摩斯是骯髒鬼，因為他把文件堆得到處都是。當他做化學實驗時，也是弄得一團亂。除此之外，他在餘暇時會拉拉小提琴，寫寫有關化學、養蜂或菸草的科學性文章。

那些認為福爾摩斯是真有其人的人，猜測他後來退隱到英國鄉間，在那裡繼續養蜂為樂！

p. 34–35

[第二章] 緊急事件

福爾摩斯問：「華生，你對這整件事有何看法？」

我回答：「依我看，這是一樁極為陰險的勾當。」

「是夠陰險的。華生，這案子非常緊急，最重要的線索是茉莉亞的遺言『有斑紋的繩子』。還有那個口哨聲和噹啷聲可能是那些吉普賽人所發出的，但我不這麼認為。來吃早餐吧，我要先進城辦事，等我回來之後我們就走。」

福爾摩斯大約一點時回來。他帶著一張藍紙，那是海倫與茱莉亞的母親的遺囑。

「史東納太太留了一萬英鎊，但兩名女孩結婚時應各拿兩千五百鎊。若她們沒結婚或先死亡，醫生可繼承所有錢財，就這一點就有殺人的動機可尋。華生，拿你的槍，我們走吧。」

我和福爾摩斯趕搭火車，我們還得租輛馬車到斯多克莫蘭。

p. 36-37　我們一到，海倫就出來了。

她苦著臉說：「我已久候多時了。」

福爾摩斯向她保證：「史東納小姐，請寬心，我們會查明的。請帶我們去看你的房間。」

海倫導引我們看各間臥室的位置。接著福爾摩斯在房屋外圍巡著，並查看了窗戶。

福爾摩斯指示海倫：「你先走進你的房間，鎖上房門。」

她鎖上房門後，福爾摩斯想打開房門，但打不開。他也試著爬窗進到屋子裡，但未能成功。

我們接著進入茱莉亞的房間，房間很小，天花板略低。福爾摩斯坐在一張椅子上四處張望，好一段時間都默不作聲。

之後他叫道：「有條鐘繩！」

一條長繩自天花板垂下。

他問她：「鐘在哪兒響呢？」

「樓下。那是用來叫喚僕人的，但我們沒有僕人，所以就沒用過。」

p. 38–39 福爾摩斯說：「這條鐘繩看起來比週遭其他東西都要來得新。」

海倫回道：「是啊，我繼父才裝了沒幾年。」

福爾摩斯看了看，拉動繩子。

「這不能用耶。瞧！它是連到通風孔的。為什麼那裡有個通風孔？通風孔應通向外面才對，但這是通到隔壁房間的，我們看仔細些。」

我們都進到醫生的房間。房間很怪異，裡頭只有三樣東西：一張床，一張木椅，還有一個鐵製保險箱。

福爾摩斯問女人：「保險箱裡有什麼？」

「我繼父的文件。」

「你繼父養貓嗎？」

福爾摩斯指著地上一個盛著牛奶的碟子。

「他只養印度豹和狒狒，那點牛奶不夠一隻印度豹喝的。」

福爾摩斯又四處巡察。他撿起一條小狗鍊，末端有個小圈。

霎時，福爾摩斯臉色更凝重了，看起來極度憂心。我們往外走，而福爾摩斯仍四處巡看了許久。

p. 40–41 「情勢很危急，你得照我吩咐你的每件事去做，這事攸關性命。」

史東納小姐點點頭。

福爾摩斯指著對街的一間小旅舍說：「我們今晚會在那間小旅舍過夜。」

「今晚，你就和昨夜一樣要待在你姊的房間。等你繼父入睡後，我要你點一根蠟燭，過一會再把它吹熄，當作給我們的暗號，然後走去你的房間等我們。我們會進入茱莉亞的房間待著。」

史東納小姐懇求：「你知道我姊的死因，是嗎？請告訴我。」

「我還未完全確定，我們得等到今晚才能確認。不能讓醫生看到我們，所以我們得走了。」

我們離開房子去小旅舍等。我們訂到一間可以朝外看到斯多克莫蘭的房間。約晚上七點時，羅伊洛特醫生回到家。我們可以聽到他在對開大門的男孩大呼小叫。

約九點時，所有燈光都熄了。我們等了約兩個多小時，看到窗子裡有閃光。

福爾摩斯說：「那是我們的暗號，走吧。」

p. 42–43 我們很快往那棟舊房子走去。一陣冷風襲向我們臉龐。我們爬過海倫事先在茱莉亞房間打開著的窗戶。我們必須非常安靜以免吵醒醫生，而我們也不敢點燈，因為羅伊洛特可能會從通風孔看到我們。

福爾摩斯低聲說：「我們不可以睡著，萬一睡著可能會沒命。」

我拿著槍以防萬一。我怎能忘掉那驚悚之夜？在那裡等待是很痛苦的，那是我這輩子最長的一夜。一小時過去了，兩小時，然後三小時。

三點時，我們從通風孔看到了一絲微光，接著是一陣嘶嘶聲。福爾摩斯感到驚恐，點了根火柴，跑去牆壁開始用力捶打。

他問我：「華生，你看到了嗎？你看到了嗎？」但我什麼都看不到。福爾摩斯點亮火柴時，我聽到了一聲低沉的口哨聲，但我看不清福爾摩斯在捶打什麼。不過我可以看到他充滿恐懼、像死人般慘白的臉。

p. 44–45 我們站著不動，一會兒就聽到一聲恐怖的尖叫，嚇得我毛骨悚然。據說下邊村莊的居民都可聽到那叫聲，我現在想到這事都還會做惡夢。

我問：「那尖叫是什麼？」

福爾摩斯告訴我：「代表這案子已破了。我們現在去醫生的房間，你的槍帶好。」

我看到了一幅奇異的畫面。我們注意到保險箱現在是打開著的，而醫生就坐在我們當天稍早看到的那張木椅上，腰腿上放著那條小狗鍊。

他死了，眼睛望著天花板。在他的頭上，我們看到了有一隻棕色斑點的黃色動物纏繞著。

福爾摩斯宣告：「那就是有斑紋的繩子。」那繩子開始動了起來，牠抬起頭，竟是一條蛇！

福爾摩斯説：「那是條從印度來的沼澤奎蛇，是印度最危險的蛇，我們把牠關回籠子吧。」

福爾摩斯撿起狗鍊往蛇的頭上纏，把蛇放進保險箱，關上門。

p. 46–47 隔天，警方説明羅伊洛特醫生因把玩危險動物而喪命。

「我看到那條連到通風孔的鐘繩時，就知道事情不對勁。羅伊洛特醫生喜歡外國動物，所以我想他或許也養了蛇。他訓練那條蛇爬過通風孔再爬下那繩子，而只要他吹口哨，蛇就會爬回來。那盤牛奶是餵蛇吃的。

醫生成功用蛇殺了茱莉亞，所以我猜他要對海倫重施故技。我一聽到那嘶嘶聲就打了下去，好讓蛇退回原處。」福爾摩斯解釋。

我說：「是啊，你打牠，牠發了火，就爬回去咬了醫生。」

「說真的，我猜我才是殺死醫生的兇手，不過我很高興受害者是他，而非海倫、你或我。」

藍寶石案

[第一章] 神秘寶石

p. 52–53

聖 誕節過後幾天，我決定去拜訪好友夏洛克·福爾摩斯。

他躺在沙發上抽著菸斗，似在沉思。我環顧房間，注意到一張椅子的椅背上有一頂非常髒的破黑帽，也注意到椅上有一支放大鏡。我猜福爾摩斯已檢視過了。

我說：「你在忙，我大概打擾到你了。」

福爾摩斯在些許片刻後終於說話了。

「完全不會。那問題很簡單，也很有趣。你知道門房彼得森這個人吧？」他問：「他發現那頂帽子，就帶來給我了，他也發現帽子旁有隻大肥鵝，他現在正在煮那隻鵝呢。」

「事情是這樣的。彼得森在聖誕節前夕去了一場派對，那派對到隔天凌晨才散。大約四點時，他在回家途中看到一個男人在他前面走著，那男人是個高個兒，手上抱著那隻鵝，頭上戴著那頂帽子。」

p. 54–55 「那高個兒走得稍遠時,一群男人突然冒出來攻擊他。他以手杖回擊,結果卻打破了身後的一扇窗,玻璃的碎裂聲嚇得他丟了鵝就跑,在打鬥中他被撞倒時帽子掉在那裡。那幫小偷也跑掉了,只剩彼得森一人,他撿起帽子,抓了鵝。」

我問:「彼得森去找了失主吧?」

「嗯,那就是問題了。我們知道失主是誰,鵝上綁了一塊牌子,上有失主姓名『給亨利・貝克太太』,帽內有 H. B. 的姓氏縮寫。我想失主想必就是亨利・貝克先生了,只不過,在倫敦,叫亨利・貝克的人這麼多呀。彼得森把帽子拿給我,可是鵝卻被他煮了。好歹牠總是要一死的。」

彼得森突然跑進來。他上氣不接下氣,結結巴巴地說道:「那鵝!鵝!我太太在鵝肚裡發現這個。」

他手中有顆漂亮的藍寶石,約一顆豆子的大小,看起來又純又亮,像星星般閃耀著。

福爾摩斯問:「我的天啊!彼得森!你知道你手中的東西是什麼嗎?」

我問:「是摩卡伯爵夫人的藍寶石嗎?」

p. 56–57 我說:「我在報紙上讀過很多有關它的報導,只要找回它就有一筆一千英鎊的可觀報酬。報上寫,伯爵夫人是在大都會飯店的住房中失竊的。警方不是已經逮到小偷了嗎?若我沒記錯,小偷叫約翰・霍納,是個水電工。其實,我這兒有那篇報導。」

福爾摩斯拿了報紙,開始大聲讀那篇文章。

大都會飯店珠寶竊案

　　當地一名叫約翰‧霍納的水電工，今日在大都會飯店因偷竊遭到逮捕。據警方表示，他從摩卡伯爵夫人的珠寶盒中偷走以藍寶石著稱的首飾品。

　　他在一名叫詹姆斯‧萊德的飯店員工提供證據指稱罪狀後，遭到逮捕。據萊德供稱，霍納受派至伯爵夫人房間修漏水，不久後，萊德被派去執行其他工作，而霍納則獨自留在房中。

　　萊德回來時，霍納已離開，伯爵夫人的梳妝檯則遭撬開，桌上的珠寶盒已空無一物。在警方的一份說明文件中，霍納曾拒捕，聲稱他是無辜的。但已判罪的霍納是最有可能的嫌犯，他將在獄中候審。

p. 58–59 福爾摩斯讀完，把報紙扔在桌上。

　　他叫著：「這只說明了警方並不了解這事，對吧？我們知道他可能是無辜的。但華生啊！我們得先弄清楚的一件事是寶石怎麼跑進鵝肚的。我們已知幾件事：這是寶石，寶石之前在鵝肚裡，而鵝是亨利‧貝克的。我們第一項工作就是找到亨利‧貝克。給我一隻筆和一張紙吧。」

　　福爾摩斯寫了如下文字：

　　某人在古吉街轉角處發現亨利‧貝克先生所擁有的一隻大肥鵝和一頂黑色軟呢帽。失主可於今晚六時三十分前來貝克街 221b 號取回。

　　福爾摩斯把那張紙遞給彼得森，說：「喏，那樣就好辦了。」

　　「聽著，彼得森先生！我要你把這訊息登在所有的晚報上，《環球報》、《星報》、《晚間新聞報》、《先驅報》，全都刊登，若還有其他報也登。」

彼得森回應：「是，先生。我馬上去辦。」

p. 60-61 我問：「我們要怎麼處理這寶石？」

「我們現在把它留在這裡。」福爾摩斯告訴我們：「彼德森！你回家時買一隻像你家人正享用的那種鵝，我們需要另一隻鵝來還給亨利・貝克先生。」

彼得森離開去辦事，福爾摩斯檢視了那寶石好一陣子。

「這寶石真是美麗啊，是吧？這就是犯罪的理由了。透光來看看它！多麼耀眼炫麗啊，只能說它真是價值非凡。這寶石問世才不過二十年左右，卻已經有一連串厄難的歷史了，它已經涉及了兩起凶殺案、一起自殺案，還引發了數宗搶案。」

福爾摩斯接著把寶石放在一個安全的地方保管好。

「我會寫信告知伯爵夫人寶石在我們這裡。」

p. 62-63 我問他：「你想水電工會是有罪還是無辜的？」

「呃，很難說。我們只能等時機到了才能找到答案。」

我問：「那亨利・貝克呢？你認為他與偷竊有關嗎？」

「我猜他對此毫不知情，但今晚他來認領鵝和帽子時我們就會知道了，到那時才會有頭緒。」

我告訴福爾摩斯：「那我要走了，我有很多事要處理，許多病人需要我看。但我對這案子的進展非常好奇，若你不介意，我會在晚上六點半前回來。」

「當然不介意了！我也想聽聽你的意見。不如你就在這裡吃晚餐吧，我們在七點開動。」

我離開福爾摩斯那裡，再回去時正好快到六點半。我走近房子，注意到有個高個兒在外面等著。我們一起進了屋子。

福爾摩斯歡迎我們一同進去，説：「我相信您就是亨利・貝克先生吧。」

那人説他是，而福爾摩斯請他坐在火爐旁。

p. 64–65 福爾摩斯問那人：「您看起來很冷。啊，華生，你來得正是時候。請問這是您的帽子嗎？」

「沒錯，正是。那隻鵝呢？」

「沒錯，那隻鵝。」福爾摩斯回答：「啊哼！是啊，那隻鵝！很可惜我們得吃了牠。」

那人驚呼：「你們吃了我的鵝！」他看起來很苦惱。

「我們得吃呀，如果我們沒吃，那隻鵝還是難逃一死。我們會還給您一隻，與先前那隻差不多大的。這隻一定可以替代已進我們五臟廟的那隻吧？」

那人回答：「當然可以！那很好。」

我和福爾摩斯對望。我們很明顯知道那人對鵝肚裡的寶石一無所知，他只是很高興有另一隻可替代他丟掉的那隻。然後福爾摩斯就去拿那人的帽子和鵝給他。

福爾摩斯説：「只是好奇一問，請問您在哪裡買到那隻鵝的？牠很好吃，我想去你買的地方再買一隻。」

「我在阿爾法酒店買的，我幾乎每晚都去。老闆開了一間鵝俱樂部，俱樂部的人每週都繳交幾便士，聖誕節時每個人就可以得到一隻鵝。福爾摩斯先生，謝謝你幫我找回鵝和帽子。」

貝克先生向我們道晚安後離去。

福爾摩斯在他離去後關上門，説：「非常謝謝亨利・貝克。」

p. 66–67 **貝克街 221b 號**

　　一名戴獵鹿帽、抽著大菸斗的男人，這幅影像能讓大部分人認出是夏洛克‧福爾摩斯。他也許是近來的文學作品中唯一能如此快速成名的角色。而福爾摩斯在倫敦的住處「貝克街 221b 號」也是一樣聞名。

　　這地址並不存在，它是道爾編造出來的。但這地址現在真實存在了！太多遊客在倫敦尋找這地址，使得英國政府終於重排街道編號，讓以前的一間宿舍變成了一間可按圖索驥的夏洛克‧福爾摩斯博物館！

　　福爾摩斯接待新客戶及與華生討論案子的起居室，看起來就像道爾的故事中描述的一樣。你可坐在火爐旁兩張椅子的其中一張上，假裝聽著福爾摩斯述說某項玄奇之謎。你也可看到福爾摩斯著名的帽子和菸斗、放大鏡、化學設備、化妝用品、許多變裝用的假髮等等。

［第二章］尋鵝記

p. 68–69 現在約晚上七點，我們原已打算在這時吃飯。

　　福爾摩斯問我：「華生，你餓了嗎？」

　　我回答：「還好。」

　　他說：「我們晚點吃，趁新線索還燙手時的趕快去追。」

　　我們換好衣服出門。夜晚酷寒，我們穿上大衣，圍上圍巾，外頭大雪紛飛，風呼呼吹著。我們呼出的氣息像煙一樣。我們很快到達阿爾法酒店，進去點了兩杯啤酒。

　　福爾摩斯向老闆說：「你的鵝很好吃，希望啤酒也好喝。」

　　老闆一臉驚訝，問：「我的鵝？」

「是啊，我聽亨利‧貝克說的，他應該是你鵝俱樂部的人。」

「噢！我懂了，那不是我們的鵝，是我從倫敦柯芬園一個肉販那裡買來的，他叫布雷肯里奇。」

我們又穿上外套，福爾摩斯說：「先生非常謝謝你。」

p. 70–71 我們又走進寒風中。

福爾摩斯扣著釦子說：「現在感謝布雷肯里奇先生。」

我們不一會兒就置身於柯芬園的市場裡。我們到處走著，終於看見一塊有「布雷肯里奇」字樣的招牌。

那老闆有張長臉。他和一個小男孩正準備關門打烊。福爾摩斯問那人：「晚安，你今晚鵝都賣光了吧？」

他回答：「你早上來可買到 500 隻。」

「不，我想買你賣給阿爾法酒店的那一批，真是好鵝啊，你是打哪兒找來的？」

這問題惹那人發起了火。

他怒氣沖沖地說：「誰都來問那鵝，聽了就煩死人了，我整天就光聽到這件事，你們八成以為世上只有那種鵝吧，搞得大驚小怪的。」

福爾摩斯說：「別人在想什麼我是不知道啦。」他的口氣聽起來好似對老闆所說的興趣不高。

p. 72–73 福爾摩斯告訴那人：「但如果你不告訴我們你鵝從哪來的，我只好不跟你打賭了。我賭五英鎊那些鵝在鄉下養的。」

「你會輸的，那些鵝是在城裡養大的。」布雷肯里奇說。

「不，我才不信。」福爾摩斯說。

「那我跟你打賭。」那人回應。

福爾摩斯大笑說：「那五英鎊我可是贏定了。」

布雷肯里奇叫那男孩：「把我的本子拿來！」

他打開本子。

「看這裡。看到沒？第 249 頁，12 月 22 日，從布里克斯頓路 117 號歐克夏太太那兒買來二十四隻鵝，每隻七先令半，以每隻十二先令賣給阿爾法酒店。所以你覺得如何呢？」

福爾摩斯假裝生氣，從口袋掏出一枚硬幣扔到桌上，氣沖沖地走出市場，我緊跟在後。

p. 74–75 當我們離開市場後，福爾摩斯開始大笑。

「你要的就這麼輕易到手了。我注意到那人喜歡打賭，因為他口袋裡有張賽馬表，我知道他抗拒不了那樣的賭注。華生，我們很快就會了結這案子。今天就到這裡，我們去吃晚餐吧。我們可以明天去拜訪歐克夏太太。」

正當福爾摩斯說完，我們聽到後面市場傳來一聲巨響，可以聽到布雷肯里奇在咆哮。我們走了進去，聽到布雷肯里奇在大吼：「滾開！我不想再聽到那些鵝，也不想在這裡再見到你！」

「嗯！我們大概不用一早去拜訪歐克夏太太了。」福爾摩斯說：「華生，我們來看看這男人是誰吧！」

我們跟著那人，在他後頭緊緊跟著。福爾摩斯碰了一下那個人的背，讓他嚇得跳了起來，臉都發白了。

他叫：「你們是誰？想幹什麼？」

「抱歉，我剛才聽到你在問鵝？我在想我也許能幫你。」

p. 76–77 他滿臉狐疑地看著福爾摩斯和我。

「你們是誰？你們跟那些鵝有什麼關係？」他問。

「這位是華生，我是夏洛克·福爾摩斯。我知道你在找已經賣給一位亨利·貝克先生的一隻鵝。貝克先生在阿爾法酒店買到那隻鵝，而阿爾法酒店又從布雷肯里奇先生那裡買來的，布雷肯里奇先生最早則是向歐克夏太太買的。」

那人的臉色一變，滿臉驚喜，大叫道：「噢！你們正是我要找的人！」

福爾摩斯說：「來我家吧。請問貴姓大名？」

那人猶豫了一下，說：「約翰·羅賓森。」

福爾摩斯平靜地問：「我想知道你的真名。」

那人面露愧色，答道：「詹姆斯·萊德。」

福爾摩斯說：「沒錯，就是你了！你在大都會飯店工作。我們就搭這輛計程車吧？到我家時我們要來好好談一談。」

那人似乎有點害怕，猶豫了一會兒要不要上車，但終究還是決定跟我們走。我們一路上都沒說話。

p. 78–79 「到了！」福爾摩斯高興地說。

「萊德先生，你看起來很冷。請坐在火爐旁……那麼，我猜你是真的很想知道你的鵝發生什麼事？」福爾摩斯問他。

「噢，是的，先生！」

「嗯，這事是這樣的，真是怪了，我以前從沒看過死鵝會下蛋，特別是下了一顆像這耀眼的藍蛋。」

福爾摩斯舉起那藍寶石。

「萊德，戲已唱完，我們在查你呢。」

那人一聽到就昏了過去。

我們給那人喝了一點白蘭地，他很快就醒了。

福爾摩斯說：「我差不多都知道了。你對霍納幹了一件大壞事。你知道他有前科，一定會被列為頭號嫌犯。你設計讓霍納進入伯爵夫人房間，再讓他背負偷竊的罪名。」

那人現時惶恐不已，懇求說：「拜託別告訴警察，我真的不是什麼壞蛋。」

「你現在被逮到了才來後悔，可是你根本不在乎霍納在獄中是不是受了苦。」福爾摩斯說。

「那這樣吧！我會出國，可是請不要告訴警察。」

p. 80-81 「告訴我們這件事的來龍去脈吧。」福爾摩斯要求。

「好吧！好吧！我偷了寶石，可是雖然警察逮捕了霍納，但我知道我不會就沒事的。我得把寶石弄走，因為警察隨時都可能來搜我。」

「於是我很快到我姊那裡去，她就是歐克夏太太，你知道她在養鵝的。在我姊那裡時，我決定去基爾伯恩。我知道有個人住在那裡，他是個罪犯，我知道他能幫我賣掉那寶石。但我還是擔心警察會在我這兒找到寶石。」

「我姊答應要送我一隻鵝，所以我就挑了一隻。我挑了一隻尾端有條紋的大鵝。我撐開牠的嘴，把寶石硬塞下牠的喉嚨，這費了我好大的勁，結果牠掙脫出我的手臂，逃回鵝群去。我又把牠抓了出來，帶到基爾伯恩去。」

「我和朋友把那鵝開腸剖肚之後，我慌了，因為裡面沒有寶石。我趕回我姊那裡，問她是否還有類似的鵝，她回答還有一隻，但問題就是她已經把那隻賣給布雷肯里奇了。接下來的你就都知道了。」

p. 82–83 我和福爾摩斯聽著他的説明。福爾摩斯沒説什麼，但表情嚴肅了起來。

突然間，他站起來摔開門，叫道：「你走吧！」

那人害怕極了，但頓時釋懷。

他説：「噢！先生謝謝你！上帝祝福你！」

那人很快跑下樓去。我們可聽到他腳步匆匆衝下樓離開。我滿懷好奇地看著福爾摩斯。

「華生，對我的工作警方從未付過一毛錢。寶石會回到伯爵夫人那裡的。萊德現在不會對霍納提出不利證明，所以他會獲判無罪開釋。萊德不會再犯錯了，所以我覺得送他進牢房沒有意義，那只會讓他的家庭陷入困難。

現在是聖誕季節，尤其是在這時節，我們要心懷寬恕。現在我想我們該來看看另一隻鵝了，希望晚餐不會又要展開另一場尋鵝之旅。」

波希米亞醜聞案

[第一章] 相片之累

p. 88–89

夏洛克・福爾摩斯一項奇特之處，是他從未對女性動心。或許，有這麼一個女人曾在他腦海中留下深深的烙印，她叫艾琳・艾德勒。他即使不算愛她，但也忘不了她。但我不會從她的事情開始描述；我會先細説一些其他的重點。

因結婚之故，我有好一段時間沒看到福爾摩斯，我決定去拜訪他。福爾摩斯非常熱情地歡迎我。

「華生！真是好久不見啊！請進！請進！你今晚順道來訪真幸運。看看這個！今天恰好收到，沒有名字、日期或地址。」

這封信短短數行，上面寫著：

某人將於今晚 7 時 45 分登門造訪，去訪之意未可明言。因眾多人士已受閣下之助，其中不乏位高之人，故本人亦望閣下能助一臂之力。

p. 90–91 他問我：「嗯，華生！你怎麼看這信呢？」

我試著學福爾摩斯思考：「信紙質感很好，我猜這人很富有，反正這是封怪信。」

「是啊。我仔細檢查後，發現紙張不是英國製的，寫信的人也許是德國人，這信紙是產自波希米亞。現在外頭有馬蹄聲，也許那就是我們的神秘訪客。」他說。

「福爾摩斯，你要我迴避嗎？」

他告訴我：「不，請留下來。我想聽你對那人來訪之意的看法。」

隨後傳來了一聲敲門響。

福爾摩斯喊：「請進！」一位神秘男子走進來。他衣著講究，臉上戴頂面具。

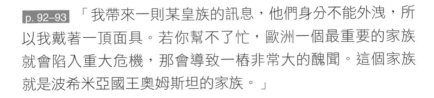

那人說：「我從波希米亞來，叫寇特·克拉姆。我來是有一件非常重要的事，你得承諾要守密。」

福爾摩斯和我應允道：「我們當然會守密。」

p. 92–93 「我帶來一則某皇族的訊息，他們身分不能外洩，所以我戴著一頂面具。若你幫不了忙，歐洲一個最重要的家族就會陷入重大危機，那會導致一樁非常大的醜聞。這個家族就是波希米亞國王奧姆斯坦的家族。」

福爾摩斯聽了後回應：「我了解的，陛下。」

那人突然嚇得跳了起來，拉下面具。

「你怎麼知道我是國王的？」那人把面具往地上丟，說：「我為何得偷偷摸摸的呢？我是國王啊。我是波希米亞國王威爾亨・奧姆斯坦。由別人處理我的事我放不下心，所以我親自來找你。」

福爾摩斯說：「請繼續說。」

「我五年前遇到一個叫艾琳・亞德勒的女人。我們……」

福爾摩斯插嘴道：「艾琳・亞德勒！1850 年出生的一位女歌手，長得很漂亮，住在倫敦。您曾愛過她吧？您寫情書給她，但後來卻離開了她。現在你想要拿回那些信。」

「是的，沒錯，而且她也有張我們的合照，我不該給她的。我那時是一個不懂事的年輕人。」國王回答。

p. 94–95 福爾摩斯問：「您試過拿回照片嗎？」

「是的，試過好幾次。」

福爾摩斯開始大笑：「她要那張照片做什麼？」

「我已訂婚要娶斯堪地那維亞國王之女珂蘿蒂爾德・羅特曼・薩克瑟─梅寧根。若她發現我與艾琳・亞德勒有關係，就不會嫁給我，但我們一定得結婚，因為我們是歐洲最重要的兩個家族。但艾琳……她很美，我離開她時她非常生氣。她不希望我去娶另一個女人，而我知道她會把照片寄給那皇族來阻止我結婚。」

「別擔心！我們會找到那照片的。我會告訴你事情的進展。」福爾摩斯向他保證。

國王在桌上放了一個袋子。「這兒是一千英鎊，我一定得拿到那張照片。這是她的地址：倫敦市聖約翰伍德區薩潘汀大道比歐尼公館。」

「陛下，晚安。」

國王離去後，福爾摩斯對我說：「明天下午三點回來這裡。」

p. 96–97 亞瑟·柯南·道爾是兇手嗎？

有關亞瑟·柯南·道爾最奇異的一件怪事，是他殺了一名同事，以替他最有名的夏洛克·福爾摩斯小說竊得構想。西元 2000 時，一位叫羅哲—加里克·斯地爾的研究者提出上述主張。斯地爾花了十一年研究道爾與另一位作家弗萊徹·羅賓森之間的關係。

據斯地爾說明，道爾很迷戀羅賓森太太，而他最有名的小說《巴斯克維爾家之獵犬》的構想正是來自羅賓森。羅賓森在一本未能順利出版的小說《達特摩爾謀殺案》中，曾描述同樣的故事。

受過醫學訓練的道爾逼他服下鴉片酊，服此毒藥會出現非常像傷寒的病狀。羅賓森死於 1907 年，得年三十，據研判死於傷寒。

當然，這論述在世上引起一陣騷動，讓福爾摩斯迷極度不滿。為了結此爭議，斯地爾嘗試取得羅賓森的遺體進行化驗。現代醫學鑑定可以證明他是否遭下毒而死，但至今尚未有結論，所以整個爭議還是一團謎——諷刺的是，這正與夏洛克·福爾摩斯的某篇故事非常雷同！

[第二章] 英雄亦有落敗時

p. 98–99

我抵達福爾摩斯住處。三點時，他人不在，但四點時有個非常奇怪的僕人進入房間，看起來又老又髒，但我隨即看出那是福爾摩斯。

我問：「你在做什麼？」

他微笑著說：「噢，華生，今天實在太有趣了。那些僕人都很願意聊聊的。我在艾琳家外頭已探得好多消息，最有趣的，就是她的律師朋友加德弗瑞‧諾頓了。我在那裡時他碰巧到達，我看著他們，但他很快就搭計程車離開了。片刻後，她也出門搭另一輛計程車跟著。」

我得跟著他們，就搭了第三輛計程車。他們去了聖莫妮卡教堂。我進入教堂，諾頓朝我喊：「快點來這裡。」

我問：「你在那兒做什麼？」

他回答：「去幫他們證婚。」

p. 100–101 我又問：「她嫁給他！那下一步是什麼？」

「呃，華生，今晚你可以不問問題就幫我嗎？」

「福爾摩斯，我當然會幫你！」

「我們晚上七點會去她在比歐尼公館的家。她請我去她家，而我要你在起居室的窗外等著，等的時候拿著這根冒煙的棍子。你看到我的手時，就把棍子丟進窗內，然後大喊：『火災啊！』不會有火災的，房間只會滿是煙霧。你完成後在街角等我。」

我說：「好啊！這我能辦到的。」

我和福爾摩斯準備著那晚的工作。福爾摩斯一改外貌，看起來判若兩人。去到她家時，我們注意到有很多人在屋外抽菸聊天。

福爾摩斯對我說：「我確定那照片在她家，我認為她不會把照片放在金庫之類的地方。我想國王的屬下只是不知道去哪裡找。」

我問：「那麼你要怎麼找呢？」

「我會等她拿給我看。」

p. 102–103 我們在說話時，一輛計程車到了。艾琳·諾頓走出了車門。就在這時，站在她家門口的那群男人突然打了起來，艾琳身處其中被推來擠去。福爾摩斯跑上前去助她脫身，但遭到圍毆。他倒在地上，臉上流了血。

這時艾琳已匆忙離去。她回頭看到福爾摩斯倒在地上。

「他受傷了嗎？」她問。

「我想他死了。」有人回答。

「他沒死，只是受傷。」另一個人說。

艾琳說：「扶他進我家。」

我看著這發生的一切，然後去起居室窗外等著。我注意看裡頭發生的事，福爾摩斯舉起手，我丟了冒煙的棍子進去，大叫：「火災啊！」那房間迅即一片煙霧。

p. 104–105 我去街角等福爾摩斯，他在約十分鐘後現身。

我問：「你拿到照片了嗎？」

他告訴我：「沒有，但她讓我看了。」

我問：「你怎麼辦到的？」

福爾摩斯只是笑著說：「我付錢給那些人在街上打架。他們扶我進艾琳家，然後你丟了冒煙的棍子進來。有火災時，人都會跑去拿他們最貴重的物品。她跑去拿照片時我就看到照片放在她的廚櫃裡。我們明天會跟國王去拿。」

福爾摩斯在我們走回他家時說著。我們走到他家門口時，有個年輕男子匆匆經過，說：「夏洛克·福爾摩斯先生，晚安。」

153

那聲音福爾摩斯很熟，他對我說：「那聲音是誰的？聲音和人我湊不起來。」

我們彼此互道晚安，約定隔天再見。

p. 106–107 一早，我們與國王一起去比歐尼公館，一名僕人在門口迎接我們，問：「您是夏洛克·福爾摩斯先生嗎？」

福爾摩斯非常驚訝，回答：「是。」

「諾頓小姐要我告訴您，她和她先生今天早上離開英國了。他們說好不會回來了。」

這項新消息讓我們震驚不已。

國王喊：「照片！不論如何都要拿到照片！」我們全部衝過僕人進到起居室。福爾摩斯打開廚櫃，裡面有張照片，但那是她的個人照。

也有一封給福爾摩斯的信，上頭寫著：

敬愛的夏洛克·福爾摩斯先生：

您的取照之計十非分善巧。火災之後，我起了疑心。我已聽說國王僱用您拿回照片，於是我便想，也許是您策畫了打鬥和火災。我扮成一個男人，跟蹤您回到您貝克街的家，以便確認。

我和我先生很快地決定離開英國。我知道國王在擔心照片，但請告訴他，我不會拿照片來威脅他的。我已經嫁給一位比國王更好的男人，所以他現在可以無牽無掛地娶斯堪地那維亞國王之女。我留下我的另一張照片，代替他想取回的那張照片。

艾琳·諾頓小姐

p. 108 福爾摩斯大聲說：「她真是冰雪聰明呀。」

國王脫口而出：「是啊，我早該娶她為妻了。」

福爾摩斯一臉凝重。

「陛下！很遺憾我沒能按計畫拿回您的照片，非常抱歉。」

「艾琳已在此信中承諾不會以照片威脅我，我相信她的諾言。我現在可以了無牽掛地娶斯堪地那維亞公主為妻，非常感謝你所做的一切。」國王告訴福爾摩斯。

「我想請求一件事。」福爾摩斯說。

「福爾摩斯先生，請說。有什麼我可以幫忙的呢？」

「我想要這唯一比我更聰明的女士的照片。」他告訴國王。

「可以，拿去吧。」

於是福爾摩斯收下了照片，而國王則娶了珂蘿蒂爾德‧羅特曼‧薩克瑟—梅寧根。

Answers

P. 48

A ① -b ② -e ③ -d ④ -a ⑤ -f
      ⑥ -c

B ① late ② wasted ③ doesn't get
      ④ the same floor ⑤ moved into her sister's room

P. 49

C ① (b) ② (a) ③ (c)

D ① sat ② told ③ sat up ④ is ⑤ live

P. 84

A ① in on -e ② up -f ③ off -d
      ④ off -b ⑤ up -a ⑥ in -c

B ① that he had never seen a dead goose lay an egg
         before
      ② that it would be an easy five pounds for him
      ③ a man he knew lived there and he was a criminal

P. 85

C ④ → ⑦ → ② → ⑥ → ③ → ① → ⑤

D ① ran off ② pick up ③ owner
      ④ problem ⑤ tag

P. 110

A ① F ② T ③ T ④ F ⑤ T ⑥ F

B ③ → ⑥ → ① → ⑤ → ② → ④

P. 111

C ① (b) ② (b)

D ① characteristic ② impression ③ description
      ④ discuss ⑤ marriage ⑥ warmly

P. 122

A
① At Christmas, everyone gets a goose. - ④
② At my sister's place, I decided I would go to Kilburn. - ⑤
③ I'll make a bet with you. - ②
④ The goose! My wife found this inside. - ③
⑤ He also found it with a large, fat goose. - ①

B
① went to ② was instructed to ③ in front of
④ there is a fire ⑤ was not able to

P. 123

C
① How did Mr. Peterson come to have the goose? (c)
② Why was the man in the market angry with Holmes and Watson? (b)
③ How did the thief end up losing the goose? (b)

D
① Holmes went to town to find an important document. (T)
② The bell-pull rang when Holmes pulled on it. (F)
③ The doctor's bedroom was nicely furnished. (F)
④ The doctor had brought exotic animals from India. (T)
⑤ At two o'clock, Holmes started hitting the wall. (F)

Adaptors of "*The Adventures of Sherlock Holmes*!"

Louise Benette

Macquarie University (MA, TESOL)
Sookmyung Women's University, English Instructor

David Hwang

Michigan State University (MA, TESOL)
Ewha Womans University, English Chief Instructor,
CEO at EDITUS

福爾摩斯【二版】
The Adventures of Sherlock Holmes

作者 _ 柯南・亞瑟・道爾爵士
　　　（Sir Arthur Conan Doyle）
改寫 _ Louise Benette, David Hwang
插圖 _ Kalchova Irina
翻譯／編輯 _ 楊堡方
作者／故事簡介翻譯 _ 王采翎
校對 _ 陳柔安
封面設計 _ 林書玉
排版 _ 葳豐
播音員 _ Michael Yancey, Tony Ross
製程管理 _ 洪巧玲
發行人 _ 周均亮
出版者 _ 寂天文化事業股份有限公司
電話 _ +886-2-2365-9739
傳真 _ +886-2-2365-9835
網址 _ www.icosmos.com.tw
讀者服務 _ onlineservice@icosmos.com.tw
出版日期 _ 2019年9月 二版一刷（250201）
郵撥帳號 _ 1998620-0 寂天文化事業股份有限公司

Let's Enjoy Masterpieces! *The Adventures of Sherlock Holmes*
Copyright ©2004 Darakwon Publishing Company
First Published by Darakwon Publishing Company, Seoul, Korea
Taiwanese Translation Copyright © Cosmos Culture Ltd. 2019

國家圖書館出版品預行編目資料

福爾摩斯 / Arthur Conan Doyle 原著；Louise
Benette, David Hwang 改編；楊堡方，王采翎翻譯．
-- 二版 . -- [臺北市] : 寂天文化，2019.09
　　　面； 公分 . -- (Grade 5 經典文學讀本)
　　譯自：The adventures of sherlock holmes
　　ISBN 978-986-318-843-8(25K 平裝附光碟片)

1. 英語　2. 讀本

805.18　　　　　　　　　　　108014312